Summer of the Burning

Summer of the Burning

FRANCES DUNCOMBE

Illustrated by Richard Cuffari

G.P. Putnam's Sons *New York*

 Published
simultaneously in Canada by Longman
Canada Limited, Toronto.
Printed in the United States of America
10214

Library of Congress Cataloging in Publication Data

Duncombe, Frances Riker, 1907-
Summer of the burning.
SUMMARY: After their house is burned down by the British and their mother dies from the effects of childbirth, a young girl finds herself responsible for keeping her younger brothers and sisters together and somehow rebuilding their home.
[1. United States–History–Revolution, 1775-1783–Fiction] I. Cuffari, Richard, 1925- II. Title.
PZ7.D914Su [Fic] 75-42956
ISBN 0-399-20513-6
ISBN 0-399-61003-0 lib. bdg.

Designed by Aileen Friedman

For Jean Fritz,
with whom I share
a love of history,
particularly that of the
American Revolution

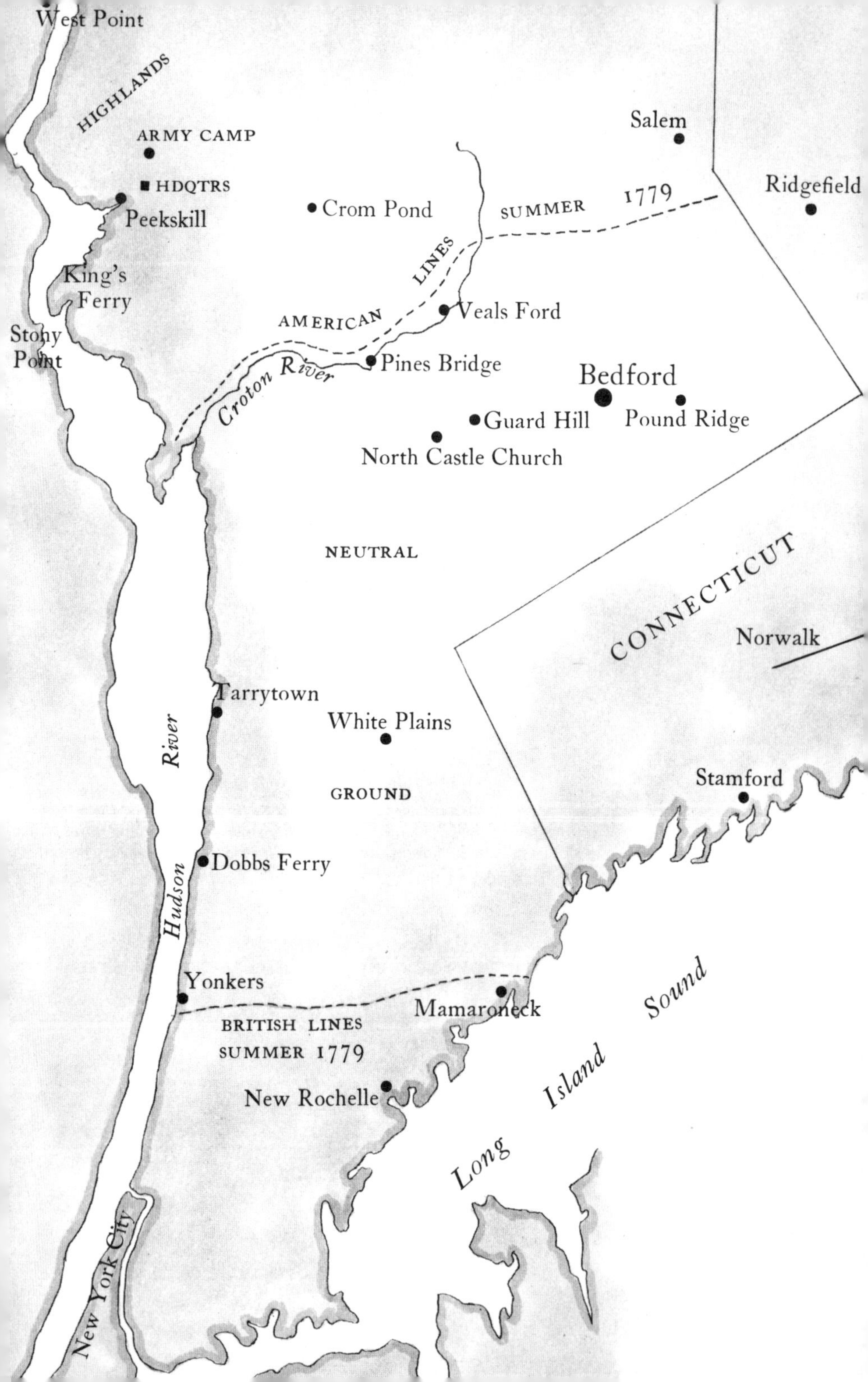

West Point
HIGHLANDS
ARMY CAMP
HDQTRS
Peekskill
Crom Pond
Salem
Ridgefield
SUMMER 1779
AMERICAN LINES
King's Ferry
Stony Point
Veals Ford
Pines Bridge
Croton River
Bedford
Guard Hill
Pound Ridge
North Castle Church
NEUTRAL
GROUND
CONNECTICUT
Norwalk
Tarrytown
White Plains
Hudson River
Stamford
Dobbs Ferry
Yonkers
Mamaroneck
BRITISH LINES
SUMMER 1779
New Rochelle
Long Island Sound
New York City

CHAPTER 1

"*And please, God, keep Pa safe and let him be exchanged real soon.*" *It was the way Hannah Mills* had ended her prayers ever since her father had been taken prisoner by the British seven months ago. But tonight she didn't end there. She went on, "And thank you, God, for sending us Moylan's dragoons." Colonel Moylan's mounted regiment hadn't yet arrived, but word had come it was on its way and would be quartered right here in the village. When it came, she could stop being scared at night.

Hannah rose from her knees and crawled into bed beside her sister, Liddy. Light filtered into the room through cracks in the floorboards of their small clapboard house facing the Common. That meant Ma was still up but the house was already locked tight for the night. So was the barn out back.

Hannah was thirteen, and sometimes it seemed as if she'd never known a time when they hadn't locked up every night. Or a time when the war hadn't been going on. Of course that wasn't really so because she had been nine when the fighting started at Lexington, up in Massachusetts, and ten before it made much difference in Bedford, New York, which was where she lived.

Then the British had taken possession of New York City and pushed up into Westchester County. They got as far as White Plains, only twenty miles south of Bedford. Pa had gone off with the militia to help the American Continentals fight against them there. Other men from the village went, too. The father of Hannah's best friend, Rachel Isaacs, was shot in the leg during the battle and still limped on account of it. Hannah had been so scared for Pa that she couldn't eat until he came back safe five days later.

Militia was local. Men like Pa and Mr. Isaacs. They were called out when there was danger close to home but seldom went beyond the county. They didn't fight outside the state the way the regular army—the Continentals—did. But Pa had been away a lot just the same, ever since the British had first set foot in Westchester.

The Battle of White Plains had been in October, 1776. Now it was July 1, 1779. In the time between, the militia had fought in many skirmishes down county and over by the Hudson River, but not in a real battle so close again. Though American troops were a familiar sight in Bedford, the British had never come that far north in inland Westchester. Hannah had never seen a British soldier. Redcoats, people called them.

It wasn't the British that they locked their doors against at night, but small bands of plundering outlaws who were terrorizing Bedford and other parts of the county that lay between the main lines of the American army on the north and those of the British on the south in the territory known as the Neutral Ground.

No one was ever really safe from these marauders except when American troops happened to be close by. Some dragoons, commanded by Colonel Elisha Sheldon, were said to be at Pound Ridge right now, but that was five miles away. Too far to be of any use. Well, Moylan would be in Bedford soon. Maybe tomorrow. Hannah closed her eyes.

Rain was pattering on the shingled roof that sloped

down over the bed. For a while it continued to fall gently. Then there was a rumble of thunder and a flash of lightning. A loud clap sounded overhead. Liddy woke and moved close.

"Hannah, I'm scared." Liddy was only five and frightened silly of thunder.

Hannah put an arm around her. "Go back to sleep, Liddy. The storm's not going to hurt us any." And to herself she added, "Should keep us safe from Cowboys and Skinners." Those were the names the outlaws went by. Cowboys if they were Tories and Skinners if they claimed to be Patriots. Hannah didn't know why.

Liddy snuggled closer. "You're sure, Hannah?"

"Real sure."

"I'm glad." Liddy sounded comforted and a moment later was asleep.

Sure? Hannah wasn't even sure the storm would keep the outlaws away. Who could ever be sure what they'd do? One night last winter, soon after Pa was captured, their barn was raided. Ma said it didn't make sense to keep on thinking about it, but as Hannah lay awake, she couldn't help remembering.

Through the low window under the eaves she'd seen lanterns moving around the barn and called for Ma to come. Together, they'd watched. It was awful. The outlaws axed down the barn door and bagged the chickens and geese and the two pigs they were planning to butcher. There was a terrible cackling and hissing and squealing. Then they drove out the cow and the horses and made off with the lot. She'd been nearly out of her mind with fear, but Ma had stayed calm. Ma always did, no matter what happened. When the raiders left, Ma only said she was glad the younger children hadn't wakened and that they'd have to get a new cow.

Now they had no livestock to steal except a few chickens and Magnolia, the new cow, but Hannah was still afraid they might come back and this time ransack the house. Some places they'd dragged people out of bed and ripped the clothes right off them and smashed everything they didn't take.

But as the storm increased, it seemed less and less likely that they'd come. Surely even Cowboys and Skinners wouldn't want to go out on a night like this with wind whipping around in the trees and branches cracking and falling.

Hannah turned onto her stomach and let her head hang over the bed. If she looked down close between the cracks in the floor, she could see her mother setting dough to rise in the room below. Though Ma was gentle and loving, she was as strong and to be depended on as that rock the pastor talked about so much. While the storm kept up and Ma was still awake, it would be safe to sleep. And tomorrow or the day after, Colonel Moylan's dragoons would be here to protect them.

During the night the thunder and lightning veered away and then returned with renewed fury. Liddy woke again and this time wouldn't be comforted. Hannah didn't get any more sleep except in fitful dozes because Liddy clung to her in terror. Then, with daylight, the storm slackened and finally ceased. Liddy relaxed her hold, and both girls drifted off into sleep, Hannah grateful that it was her brother Elijah's morning to milk.

Waking with sunlight in her eyes, Hannah heard her six-year-old brother, Andrew, talking excitedly. His words came up loud through the floor.

"Ma, he said there were hundreds, maybe thousands. This morning before it was light."

"Who said?" Elijah's voice was condescending. "And thousands of what?" Elijah was eleven but liked to be taken for older.

"The black boy from the tavern told Aaron, and

Aaron told me. Just now. So there!" Aaron Isaacs was Andrew's best friend, just as Rachel Isaacs was Hannah's, and his word was not to be disputed.

Elijah sounded as though he were getting ready to break in when Ma stopped him. "Wait, son, let your brother finish."

"Soldiers on horses," Andrew went on. "Hundreds or thousands or maybe millions. From Guard Hill way. They went right past the meetinghouse and tavern and on up the Ridgefield road."

"Colonel Moylan." Ma sounded as though she was smiling, and Hannah guessed she was subtracting quite a few soldiers. "He must have missed the turn in the storm. He'll be back."

"More likely he's not going to stay in Bedford after all," Elijah said pessimistically. "Likely his orders were changed. Maybe he's gone on to Ridgefield. Or maybe turned off the Ridgefield road beyond Indian Hill and gone to Pound Ridge."

Hannah slid out of bed quietly so as not to wake Liddy and pulled her dress over her head. Without stopping to fasten all the buttons, she ran downstairs. In the big dark-beamed and whitewashed room below, her mother was putting loaves of raised dough into the chimney oven to bake. Ma's figure was bulky because a baby was coming soon, but she was tall and big-framed anyway and didn't show nearly as much as Rachel's mother, who was also expecting. Ma was blue-eyed and had hair the color of honey just like the young ones, Andrew and Liddy. Elijah was dark the way Grandma Mills had been and big for his age. But Hannah took after Pa all the way. Her eyes were green, and her hair was sandy, and she was small and wiry the way he was.

"Morning, Hannah." Ma gave her a smile. "It seems Moylan's dragoons came by before daylight this morning and went right on, north of us. Missed the way, but they'll be back as soon as they find out their mistake."

"Yes, Ma, I heard from upstairs." Hannah knew her mother had been counting on the safety the dragoons would give the village, too, but she wasn't letting on she was worried.

"Perhaps he didn't go far," Hannah offered. "He could have gone up Indian Hill. Perhaps he's going to make camp for the men up there."

Indian Hill lay just east of the village between the Ridgefield road and the south road to Pound Ridge that ran past their house. Its top was a wide high plateau, sloping gently down on the north. On the south it descended by precipitous cliffs.

"Can I go see, Ma? Can I?" Without waiting for an answer Andrew dashed off, followed by Elijah.

"Better go too, Hannah," Ma said. "Keep them from getting underfoot if Moylan is really there setting up camp."

"Yes, Ma," Hannah replied. Even if the boys did get in the way, she couldn't do much about Elijah. He never paid attention to anything she told him. But it would be no use saying so. Especially now when she was in a hurry to get to Indian Hill herself and find out about Moylan.

CHAPTER 2

The Mills' house was south of the Common, on what since the town's first days had been called the Street. Running east, it skirted Indian Hill and became the Pound Ridge road. The other end swung south and led to White Plains. Hannah's great-grandfather had helped lay out the Street in 1681. The village, too, with its three-acre home lots and the burying ground at the edge of the Common where the first Presbyterian meetinghouse had stood. Bedford was the oldest and prettiest village for miles around. Mostly two-story houses, either shingled or white clapboard, yards with flowers front and side, fruit trees out back by the barns and outbuildings. Hannah couldn't imagine living anywhere else.

The Isaacs' house was almost next door to the Mills', and as Hannah passed it, she found Rachel waiting for her.

"The boys have gone on. Aaron is with them," she told Hannah. "Let's hurry." She started to run.

Less than half a mile from the Common the ground on the north side of the road became steep cliffs. It was possible to climb straight up in places but quicker as well as safer to take the trail that led upward on a zigzag course a little farther on. Folks said that years ago there had been a large Indian village on the broad plain at the top of the cliffs. Certainly there was room enough up there for an Indian settlement. More than enough for a regiment of dragoons.

Halfway up the path was a flat rock, and the girls stopped to rest and catch their breath. They'd lost sight of the boys before they started climbing and hadn't heard their voices for some time.

Far below them a man on horseback galloped toward Bedford.

"Wonder what he's in such a hurry about?" Rachel put up a hand to shade her eyes. Rachel had big dark eyes and dark curling hair. Often Hannah wished she was pretty like Rachel, even when Ma said it didn't matter so long as she was good.

Both girls watched until the horse turned a bend in the road before they started climbing again.

When they finally reached the top of the cliffs and came out into a high field of sparse grass, there was nothing moving as far as they could see. Hannah turned her eyes to the ground. "Manure," she said, "but a week old at least. If there are horses up here, they must be on the other side."

Ahead, the field rose gently until it met the sky. Before they reached the crest, Elijah appeared over it, coming toward them. Andrew and Aaron tagged along in his rear.

"Moylan's not here anywhere," Elijah told Hannah, making it sound as though it were her fault somehow. "They've gone on like I said."

"They'll come back," Hannah insisted, but the others sided with Elijah.

"Might as well go home." Andrew kicked at the ground in disgust. Suddenly he sniffed, then threw himself full length in the grass.

"Wild strawberries," he announced delightedly, "lots and lots and lots."

Under leaves that hid them until at their own level

little ripe berries grew three to four on a stem. Sugar was so scarce in Bedford that few people had any. Honey was dealt out meagerly. But here unexpectedly was sweetness in abundance.

Disappointment was for the time forgotten. No one cared that the grass they were lying or kneeling on was still wet or noticed when it wasn't wet anymore because the sun was higher and had grown hot. At last Hannah couldn't eat even one more berry.

"I'm full," she said blissfully, licking her fingers. She knew they should go home to waiting chores. But she didn't want to hurry or to hurry anyone else. It was so lovely up here on Indian Hill with the air clear after last night's storm and the sky high and blue.

She walked to the top of the crest and stood waiting for the others. She could see for miles today. To the northwest she could even make out the purplish outlines of the Hudson River Highlands.

Once Jacob, Rachel's older brother, had explained why defense of the Hudson was so important that little protection could be spared for inland Westchester. He said if the British could take the big fort at West Point, they'd get to control the whole river and could sail right up past Albany. He said it would cut the American army in half and General Washington would have to give up.

Jacob was tall and big-boned and strong as an ox. But after the war he planned to study and be a teacher. Hannah was sure he knew what he was talking about. Only Bedford was important and needed protection, too! Without it Cowboys and Skinners had everything their way. Well, now it seemed Washington thought the same. He'd sent them Moylan's dragoons. Moylan had missed the turn at the crossroads, but he'd be back.

Hannah turned away from the Highlands to look up the Ridgefield road, and as if to prove her right, a column of cavalry was coming down it. The road was half a mile below the crest of Indian Hill, but there was no doubt in Hannah's mind.

"Rachel," she called, "come quick. It's Moylan's dragoons! They're coming back!"

Rachel came running, and so did the boys.

Aaron looked for almost a minute without speaking. Then he said, "The horses in the middle are cows."

Elijah laughed, and in spite of herself, Hannah joined in, but Andrew shouted angrily, "They are too cows. If Aaron says so, they are!"

The moving line disappeared, hidden by a sharp dip in the road as it approached Bedford.

"Let's get back in a hurry!" Rachel cried.

"Wait, there's more coming," Aaron said. About a mile behind the first column came a second, riding much faster.

The cliffs were still the shortest way back, and everyone dashed for them. They slipped and slid, but finally they all were safe at the bottom. Then they ran. They expected to be outdistanced to the crossroads by the horses. What they didn't expect was to find their way blocked by cattle. Part of the Common fence was broken down, and both the Common and the street east of it were filled with strange cows and steers. They were mooing and bawling and milling around where they had no business to be.

"Aaron was right," Andrew said, but no one, not even Aaron, paid attention. They were pushing toward the north end of the village where they could hear excited shouting. No one could want a louder welcome, Hannah thought as she ran forward. It wasn't until she was quite close that she saw that this was no welcoming party.

There was no sign of mounted troops. The shouting crowds were beating at flames. Both the tavern that belonged to Rachel's uncle, Saul, and the meetinghouse were on fire.

CHAPTER 3

Behind swirls of smoke at the north end of the village Hannah could see people moving and hear them shouting. At first she couldn't recognize anyone. Then the breeze shifted. She saw her mother come out of the meetinghouse, carrying one end of a heavy bench while the pastor carried the other.

"Let me take it, Ma," she called as she pushed toward them, but Ma wouldn't let her end go.

"There's need of water," she said. "Get a bucket from the horse shed."

Hannah's eyes searched the smoke for Moylan's dragoons. Where were they? Why weren't they helping? She grabbed a bucket and ran toward the stream behind the tavern where boys and girls were filling buckets and running back with them to the burning buildings.

"What happened?" she asked Rachel, who was beside her at the stream. "Have you heard?"

"No," Rachel replied and ran off, water sloshing onto the ground.

"What happened?" Hannah repeated the question to Jacob Isaacs as she put her filled bucket into his outstretched hands. He dashed the water through a broken window of the tavern, where it hissed and sent up a white cloud of steam.

"British." He dropped Hannah's bucket and reached for another that was being offered.

British? British had come to Bedford? Hannah felt as though Jacob had thrown the water at her instead of into the flames. She'd never thought they'd come. She wouldn't have believed it now except Jacob always got things straight.

"Is Moylan chasing them?" she shouted against the sharp crack of a beam falling, but Jacob didn't take time to reply.

After that, Hannah didn't have breath enough to ask questions. She made the trip to the stream again and again and again. She ran until her legs ached. She carried until her right arm felt longer than her left. Just as she knew she couldn't make even one more trip, it was all over. The tavern roof collapsed in a shower of fiery sparks, and the wall fell in. Only the chimney was left standing in a heap of water-soaked smoldering ashes and charred bits of lumber. They'd been able to save the meetinghouse across the road.

Then Hannah found her mother. Ma said Moylan hadn't come. She said Sheldon's troops from Pound Ridge had chased the British out of Bedford, and they'd let the cattle they'd stolen at Pound Ridge go. But Ma said it was only what she'd heard and people told different stories.

When the danger of flames breaking out again seemed over, people started going home. Hannah saw Ma start home with Andrew and Liddy. Rachel's mother stopped to say a few consoling words to Mr. Saul Isaacs on the loss of his tavern, and then she followed.

Hannah and Rachel sat down on the trampled grass in front of the meetinghouse to watch for sparks. Their eyes were smarting, and their faces blackened.

A slim blond girl was standing a few feet off.

"Come and sit with us, Tamar," Rachel invited. The girl glanced hesitantly at Hannah.

Hannah started to turn her head away. Once she and Tamar Halstead had been friendly, but not since Pa had been taken by the British. It wasn't just because the Halsteads were still loyal to the king—there were other Tories in Bedford, and so long as they stayed quiet and didn't cause any trouble, no one paid them much attention. There was more to it. Tamar's uncle Roger wasn't peacefully minding his farm anymore. He'd left Bedford and joined De Lancey's Refugees, the most hated Tory troop in all of Westchester. And he'd done it the very same week they'd heard Pa had been put in the Sugar House Prison in New York City.

Rachel said it wasn't fair to hold this against Tamar. Even Ma said so, but Hannah couldn't help how she felt. Sometimes, though, she felt ashamed. She did right now because Tamar had been fighting the fire as hard as she and Rachel, even though it had been started by the British. So instead of turning away, Hannah moved over and made a place beside her on the grass.

With a quick shy smile, Tamar walked over and joined them. "I'm sorry about your uncle Saul's tavern," she said to Rachel, "but there wasn't any hope of saving it. Even at the very beginning."

"Were you here when they came?" Rachel's eyes brightened with interest.

"Yes," Tamar said. She looked as though she didn't want to talk about it, but Rachel prodded her.

"Then tell us what really happened. Everything."

Tamar put a hand up to her forehead to shove away a strand of hair, and Hannah saw a nasty burn on her elbow.

"Better go home and get that fixed," she suggested, but Tamar shook her head. "I've got to stay until I'm sure the last spark is dead," she replied.

"Go on about the fire," Rachel pressed.

"All right." With her eyes on the still smoldering ruins of the tavern, Tamar began slowly, knowing Rachel would never let up until she had told everything she knew.

"About seven-thirty a messenger came galloping in and called out there was fighting at Pound Ridge and that every man in the militia was needed even if his term of enlistment was up. They all grabbed their muskets and left on the run."

"I guess it was the messenger that we saw from halfway up Indian Hill," Rachel put in.

"Well, anyway after the men left, the rest of us just waited, not knowing what was going on and scared. Then the British came. Down the Ridgefield road."

"We saw them, too," Hannah said, "only they were too far away to see their red coats. We thought they were Moylan's dragoons."

"Most weren't wearing red," Tamar told her. "Someone said they were Tarleton's British Legion with part of the 17th Light Dragoons and some Hessians and Queen's Rangers. Tarleton was in command."

"Then what happened?" Rachel asked impatiently.

Tamar shivered. "I was right there by the meetinghouse. I hardly had time to get out of the way." She stopped, and for a minute it seemed she wasn't going to say anything more. Then she continued, speaking in short, jerky sentences.

"They came through with a big bunch of cattle. The officer who was commanding them stopped and set fire to the meetinghouse. Then somebody shot at him from the tavern. He told his men to forget the meetinghouse and throw brands in every window of the tavern. Then Sheldon's men came chasing after them from Pound Ridge. The British let the cattle loose and made off up the Guard Hill road. Sheldon followed. That's all I know."

She got up to trample on a spark and didn't come back to join the other girls again.

Rachel left soon afterwards, and Hannah started home. She'd only gone a short ways from the crossroads when she heard her name called and looked back.

"Hannah." It was Major Tallmadge, Sheldon's second-in-command. He'd been a friend since last summer when he'd stabled his horse in their barn for a while. Only it wasn't the same horse as the exhausted-looking animal he was leading now.

The major looked bone-tired, too, and the sleeve of his blue jacket was slashed and dark brown around the slash. Blood.

"Oh, sir, you're hurt!'" Hannah cried.

"Just a scratch," the major replied. "I got it at Pound Ridge when they captured my horse."

Hannah looked at the animal he was leading. "Borrowed," he said, "to chase after Tarleton. But she fell twice from exhaustion, and I had to drop out. They won't catch him anyway."

"What happened at Pound Ridge, sir? No one here knows. Is it all right to ask?"

The major took off his heavy helmet and wiped the sweat from his forehead.

"It's no secret, Hannah. Only I'm not sure how to answer you. Tarleton will say he won because he set a few fires and captured our regimental standard and baggage. Sheldon will say we won because we were outnumbered but our regiment wasn't cut to pieces. And in the end Tarleton left. Both sides took a few prisoners. So take your choice." He sounded a little bitter. "It's generally that way in skirmishes between mounted troops."

Then his voice changed. "But about the mare, Hannah. She can't go any farther right now. Can I leave her in your barn for an hour or so?"

"I'm sure Ma would want that," Hannah said, "and I'll rub her down and cool her for you if you like. The way you showed me last summer."

"I'd be grateful," Tallmadge said. "I'll be by for her later."

Hannah put the reins over her arm and started leading the mare off. She'd only gone a few steps when Tallmadge called to her again. "Wait, Hannah. Have you news of your father? Has an exchange been arranged yet?"

She shook her head, but she didn't look around. She knew she was going to cry and she didn't want anyone, not even a friend like the major, to see her crying. She wished she was brave like Ma, but she wasn't. She had never seen Ma cry. Not even when they first heard Pa had been imprisoned at the Sugar House.

Half blinded by tears mixed with soot, Hannah led the mare toward home. On reaching the barn, she took off the saddle and rubbed the mare's wet coat with hay. Then she walked her around and rubbed her some more before putting her into a stall and giving her a little water in the bottom of a bucket.

When she finished, she felt better. Pa would be all right, just as Ma said, and an exchange might come sooner now because of the British captured at Pound Ridge.

Late in the afternoon, when Hannah went to the Common to bring Magnolia in for milking, the stolen cattle had already been sorted out and driven back to Pound Ridge. Rachel was waiting. She had come to fetch the Isaacs' cow, but she seemed in no hurry. She was reading names on the tombstones that stood in rows at the southwest corner. She turned as she heard Hannah approach.

"I'm glad we will be buried here," she said seriously. "We moved a lot before coming to Bedford." Then an anxious look suddenly showed in her eyes. "Will it matter that we're Jews?"

"Of course not," Hannah said. "The burying ground is for everyone, not just Presbyterians."

Rachel gave a sigh of relief. "I'm glad. I never thought to ask before. I don't want anyone in our family buried just yet, but it must make a person feel more—more a part of Bedford to have folks buried here with stones to show their names and when they were born and died. I want my children to feel that way."

"Your children!" Hannah couldn't keep from laughing.

"Yes, my children." Rachel's voice was steady and determined. "I intend to marry someone who lives right here."

"But, Rachel! You're only thirteen. It's silly to talk about marrying."

"Almost fourteen," Rachel corrected, "and Major Lockwood's daughter is only fifteen and she's married and having a baby."

Hannah gave in. "Well, then, who will you marry?"

"Tamar's brother, maybe. He likes me."

"You can't. He's a Tory!"

"Well, maybe I won't. Or maybe I will." With a giggle her mood changed. "*You* can marry Jacob," she teased.

"Jacob doesn't even look at me except when I'm with you and he's explaining things or telling us what we should do," Hannah protested.

"Why should he?" Rachel asked reasonably. "Right now his mind is mostly on getting to be sixteen and joining the militia."

Hannah felt herself growing annoyed and embarrassed. She admired Jacob, but what Rachel was saying was silly. Jacob wouldn't like it either. Just imagining what he'd think if he heard made her blush. She left the burying ground and went off to get Magnolia, who was grazing contentedly across the Common. Slapping her on the rump, she said, "Come on, cow, it's time we got home."

Leaving, she called back, "Bye now, Rachel. I'll see you after supper. Ma wants me to bring a present over."

CHAPTER 4

Major Tallmadge's horse was gone when Hannah brought Magnolia in from the Common. Elijah and Andrew were collecting eggs in the hen house attached to the barn, and she could hear them arguing.

"They'll come again now they know the way. It only stands to reason." Elijah sounded as though anyone who disagreed with him must be witless.

When she opened the top of the long wooden feed bin, Magnolia mooed, and Andrew knew she was back. He came running to her.

"Hannah, they won't come again. Tell Elijah so," he begged. But Elijah had already started up to the house with the eggs.

"Get Tabby's bowl, Andrew," Hannah said to turn his mind on something else. When he brought the cat's bowl, she pulled on one of Magnolia's teats and aimed a stream of milk into it. Then she drew up the three-legged stool Pa had made last summer and settled to milking. Magnolia was an easy milker and stood quiet so there was no need to think about her kicking over the bucket or anything.

Ever since morning people had been arguing the same as Elijah and Andrew. Hannah didn't know which to believe. Even now the hardest thing to believe was that the British had been in Bedford at all.

At supper Elijah was still wanting to talk about how the British would come back. Ma tried to stop him by shaking her head and then nodding toward the young ones, Andrew and Liddy. But he didn't catch on, so she said right out, "That's enough talking, Elijah. Major Tallmadge said Tarleton aimed to capture Sheldon's dragoons before Moylan got here. Well he didn't, and he can't try again till his horses get rested up. Before then, Moylan will be here. So you see there's no more danger and no sense going on about it."

Elijah scowled because he didn't like Ma shutting him up, but Andrew's face brightened. He'd been worrying. So had Hannah, but now she knew what to believe. The same as Ma. There was no more danger from the British and no sense going on about it.

After supper Hannah went over to the Isaacs' to take the present Ma had made for the baby they were expecting.

Rachel was in the room the Isaacs' had added on when they'd bought the house. It had papered walls and a flowered rug on the floor. Her uncle, Saul, was there telling about Tarleton setting fire to the meetinghouse and his tavern. Rachel's father hadn't been in Bedford when it happened. He was a purchaser for the American Commissary Department, and he'd only just got home from a trip. Now he was listening and nodding his head.

Mrs. Isaacs wasn't paying much attention to the men. She sat at a small round table near the window, sewing on some fine white material. When she saw Hannah, she smiled and held up a tiny dress. She was putting lace around the neck.

"It's for the new baby coming to your house," she said.

Hannah had never seen anything so pretty. When Ma made clothes for a new baby, they were of unbleached muslin. She almost felt ashamed now that Ma's present

to Mrs. Isaacs was a muslin shirt. But when she gave it to her, Mrs. Isaacs said a shirt was just what she needed most and she'd never seen featherstitching done so fine.

All the while Hannah's eyes had been glued to the little dress. "It's just beautiful," she said. "Ma will use it for the christening. I know she will."

"I am hoping so." Mrs. Isaacs went back to sewing on lace, and Hannah went over and sat on a bench with Rachel near her father and uncle.

"Saul, we want you to share our house until you can rebuild the tavern," Rachel's father was saying.

"No, David, though thank you kindly," her uncle replied. "We've taken rooms where we can keep our eyes on the outbuildings. They are filled with the things we managed to save."

Then Mr. Isaacs asked, "How do you think the British knew Sheldon was at Pound Ridge?" Hannah leaned forward so as not to miss a word.

"Some say Halstead told."

Tamar's father! So that's what people thought!

Mr. Isaacs sighed and pulled at his beard. "It's going to be hard to get that next drove of cattle through to the army at Peekskill. Tories are informing everywhere and British and Refugees are raiding as bad as Cowboys over by the Hudson."

"Papa, when is the next cattle drive going to be? Can I go, too? I could help." Rachel was so exicted that she spoke right out. Mr. Isaacs looked up as though he'd forgotten she was there.

"No, Rachel, and it's time for you to find Aaron and bring him in to bed." Hannah could tell from the way he spoke that he wanted to get rid of them both, but Rachel kept at it.

"I ride better than Jacob. If he goes, why can't I?"

"Jacob is near sixteen, and he's a boy. That's why. Now do as I tell you." Mr. Isaacs had begun to sound angry. Rachel knew better than to answer back, but when they got outside the house, she exploded.

"That Jacob! He can do anything he wants. Just because he's a boy."

Hannah started to say good-night when Andrew and Aaron came racing around the corner of the house. Hannah caught Andrew and took him home to Ma. Then she went down to the barn to lock up.

It was quiet in the barn. The chickens had gone to roost, and Magnolia's tail made a soft sleepy-sounding swish as she swung it against her rump and flanks to keep the flies off. Soon it would be dark. Hannah wished Major Tallmadge hadn't taken his horse yet so he'd come back later on. She wasn't worrying about the British coming back. Ma had said they wouldn't. But there would be another scary night of wondering about Skinners or Cowboys because Moylan hadn't come either.

Only she didn't stay awake long wondering. She was so tired after all that running and carrying at the fire that she went right to sleep as soon as she got to bed. And didn't wake up when there was a knock on the door. She didn't wake until Ma shook her real hard.

"Hannah," she said, still shaking her, "get up."

It was still dark so Hannah knew it wasn't time to milk. It had to be outlaws. If there was warning, Ma always made her take Magnolia to the woods and hide her. She hated hiding with Magnolia at night. It was spooky.

"No, Ma, please. Elijah is old enough. Send him this time," Hannah begged, but she was already on her feet.

"Elijah?" Ma sounded confused. "Send Elijah? To a birthing? You must be daft or dreaming. Mrs. Isaacs has started her pains and sent Jacob to say I should come. I need you to lock the door behind me when I leave."

Hannah didn't go back to bed when Ma left. She

wanted to be right there to hear her special knock on the door the minute it came. She wanted to know right away whether the Isaacs' baby was a boy or a girl. It seemed a long time waiting, but she knew everything would be all right because no one was better at bringing babies than Ma. At last the knock came, and Hannah drew back the bolt and opened up. Ma was standing on the step and smiling.

"An easy birth," she said before Hannah had time to ask. "It's a fine little boy. They are naming him Benjamin."

CHAPTER 5

The day after little Ben Isaacs was born Moylan's dragoons marched into Bedford. There was no mistake about it this time. Around midmorning a man on top of Guard Hill saw them coming and sent his son galloping into the village with the news. All at once it seemed as though everyone was shouting "MOYLAN" and running out of their houses toward the crossroads. Hannah saw Mrs. Baylor, the short heavyset woman from next door, hurrying along with her four boys. Mrs. Slawson, the neighbor on their other side, was trying to keep up with her own boy and two little girls, who were running on ahead. Ma had hold of Liddy and kept calling to Andrew and Aaron Isaacs to wait.

Elijah and Eben Baylor, who was his age, climbed right to the top of the big oak on the corner. They were so high up Hannah could scarcely see them because of all the leaves between them and the ground, but Elijah hollered down that they had a fine view and dared Andrew to climb up to where they were. Ma wouldn't let him, so he and Aaron climbed a maple that wasn't so tall. Pretty soon all the trees were as full of boys as they were of crows at corn-planting time, and just as noisy.

Rachel was on the roof of the meetinghouse shed. "Come on up here with us," she called. "It's a fine place if you're careful of splinters."

The "us" was Rachel and Tamar. Hannah wished it was just Rachel, but on a day like this with everyone feeling so good about Moylan coming, she didn't mind too much.

The shed backed up against a bank, so it wasn't hard to get up on the almost flat roof. Hannah sat down beside Rachel and Tamar, and they all looked west up the Guard Hill road. Tamar wasn't usually much of a talker, but happy to be with the other girls, she was chattering now like a magpie. She asked Rachel how their baby was doing, and then she asked Hannah when theirs was coming. Hannah looked down at Ma, who was holding onto Liddy, and hoped it would be soon. The Isaacs' baby was a healthy one, and Mrs. Isaacs had let her hold him. They hadn't had a baby of their own that lived since Liddy, and she'd forgotten how sweet they were. She could hardly wait for theirs to get born, but she was worried, too. With Pa not home, she wondered what she'd do if things didn't go right the way Ma said they would.

They were still talking about babies when suddenly Elijah hollered, "I see them!" and Eben yelled, "I do, too! They're on this side of Guard Hill!"

Everyone started cheering. The girls stood up, but the roof wasn't high enough to see anything. A while after that someone shouted, "Silence," loud enough to stop the noise.

Then everyone heard, or it was more like feeling than actually hearing at first. The way you feel the beat of drums. Only this was hoofbeats. The steady, pounding hoofbeats of cavalry on the march. Hannah's heart began to thump, and her throat choked up. She looked around at Rachel and knew she felt the same. Tamar was standing still with tears streaming down her cheeks.

They still couldn't see anything. Then Rachel grabbed Hannah and said, "Look!" Five dragoons had come up fast and were so close they could see the color of the horses. The rest were coming on more slowly, but now they could see them, too. A trumpet sounded, and the main body of the regiment halted.

The waiting was almost more than they could bear. They'd seen light horse troops often before. Sheldon's had been around most of last summer, sometimes in one place and sometimes in another. But this regiment was different. It was to stay right in Bedford. It was here to protect them.

When the advance guard rode into the village, Rachel leaned so far out over the shed roof that Hannah was scared she'd fall off.

"I'm choosing that sergeant," she said, "so both of you just keep your eyes to yourselves."

Hannah knew she was joking, so she said she'd rather wait for a lieutenant. Tamar didn't say anything, and Rachel asked who she was going to choose. She still didn't answer, so Rachel teased her about holding out for a captain.

Then Tamar did answer, but she wasn't joking like the others. "Please stop, Rachel," she said. "No Continental soldier would look at me and you know it."

It was true, of course. Not with what people were saying about her father. For a moment they all just stood there, tongue-tied and awkward. Then Tamar jumped down from the roof and ran off into the crowd. They saw her join her brother Elliott, a tall, slight boy of fifteen.

Rachel said, "Oh, Hannah, that was awful of me. I should have thought. I never should have started that stupid game!"

Hannah felt bad, too. No matter how she felt about Tamar, she didn't want her hurt. Especially when everyone else was feeling so excited and happy. But the next minute both girls forgot about her.

The sergeant and the four dragoons he led had separated, each riding toward a different road that came into the village. Now the sergeant was galloping back to the waiting troops. Again a trumpet called, and the regiment moved forward. It was a wonderful sight. The dragoons rode four abreast, taking up the whole width of the road. They came on, row after row of them in high fur caps above green jackets. When they reached the crossroads, everyone went wild, and even after hours of marching, the horses acted up a little.

Colonel Moylan was at the head of the column in front of the standard. He doffed his high dragoon cap and bowed right and left as he tried to make his way through the crowd, but people closed in around him, and he had to stop or trample them. So he reined in his horse, and the column halted behind him. Everyone got a good look then. Though as old as Pa, Hannah thought Colonel Moylan was the handsomest man she'd ever seen. When he spoke, his voice had a rich warm sound they later learned was Irish.

"I thank you for this kindly welcome," he said, smiling. "When the regiment is properly settled, I shall look forward to receiving any of you who may choose to call. If you have any complaints against my men, they will be dealt with promptly and firmly. As you know, we will be quartered right here in Bedford with orders from General Washington to protect this place and its inhabitants."

It was what everyone wanted to hear from his own lips. There was loud cheering and then the crowd stepped out of his way and let him go.

Colonel Moylan chose as his headquarters the biggest house on the street east of the Common, the house next to Tamar's. Some of his officers were quartered there with him; some at other houses. The privates and noncommissioned officers set up camp in the big flat meadow between the Street and the river, leaving a piece on one side for a parade ground. The horses were there, too, except those belonging to officers.

Ma had left the crossroads as soon as Colonel Moylan finished talking because Liddy was tired and hungry. When Hannah got back home, two officers were in front of the house talking to her mother while their horses nibbled at the grass. Ma introduced the handsome red-haired one as Lieutenant O'Malley and the dark-haired one as Lieutenant Smith. They asked Ma if she had any room in the barn, and when she said yes, they offered to pay for stabling their horses. Hannah said she'd feed and water them if they wanted, and they said they'd pay for that as well. When they were leaving, after showing Hannah how to do things the way they wanted, Rachel strolled by. Her face was perfectly innocent, but her eyes were too innocent. Hannah knew she was remembering the silly thing she'd said about waiting for a lieutenant.

CHAPTER 6

Hannah stretched her legs out toward the bottom of the bed, careful not to touch Liddy and rouse her. It was still dark, but she wasn't longing for daylight. It was blissful to lie awake, knowing the village was safe and that tomorrow Moylan's dragoons would still be around in their spick-and-span uniforms and shiny spurs. The fear of raiders she'd lived with so long was gone. Even her worry about Ma was gone. And that was because of the dragoons, too. Ma had kept on saying that everything was going to be all right when she had the baby. That likely she'd not even need any help. But just the same, when it started coming Hannah should find Elijah and send him to fetch old Mrs. Woolsey, who lived north of the village.

Mrs. Woolsey was so dirty that Hannah hated to think of her touching Ma and the baby. But Ma said there was no choice. Since Mrs. Bracket had moved away, the only people in Bedford skilled in bringing babies were Mrs. Woolsey and herself.

Well, now there was a choice. A couple of days after Moylan came, Hannah was down at the barn with Lieutenant Smith. Right from the first he had been like a brother, so it seemed natural for him to ask if Ma had anyone in mind to bring the baby. Lieutenant Smith was brushing Dandy before saddling and riding out, and

Hannah was brushing Dolly because Lieutenant O'Malley was late. She kept on working for almost a minute before she replied. She knew Ma wouldn't want her to say anything against Mrs. Woolsey. It would be almost like disobeying Ma to say how she felt, but Lieutenant Smith had been kind to ask, and she'd have to make some answer.

"Yes, Ma has someone in mind." That was all she'd meant to say. But then words gathered in a rush and she couldn't stop them. "It's Mrs. Woolsey. She's that old woman who looks like a witch with a beaky nose and long, greasy hair. She's the dirtiest woman in Bedford."

Lieutenant Smith looked distressed and puzzled. "Why is your mother having her then? I don't understand."

"Because there's no one else, that's why," Hannah said miserably.

Smith put down Dandy's brush and walked over to her. "But there is someone, Hannah. That's why I asked."

"There is?" Suddenly the weight of worry lifted. "Who is she?"

"He, Hannah. The surgeon for the regiment, and he's right up the street in the house with O'Malley and me."

"A doctor!" Hannah exclaimed. "Doctors don't deliver babies!"

"But they do, Hannah," Lieutenant Smith told her. "Doctors in Pennsylvania, where our regiment comes from, have been taught midwifery for over ten years. Our surgeon says he's delivered a good many babies."

"Do you think he'd be willing?" Hannah asked eagerly.

"Yes, I do," the lieutenant replied.

"Then I'll tell Ma! I'll tell her right away!" Abandoning O'Malley's mare, Hannah flew up to the house.

At first Ma said she'd have to think about it. Having

a man instead of a woman would be a strange thing. Then after a little she said she would talk to the surgeon.

That evening Lieutenant Smith brought the surgeon over, and he and Ma talked alone. When he left, Hannah could hardly wait to find out what Ma thought.

"Did you like him, Ma? Did you?" she asked.

"Yes, I did," Ma said. "It was a pleasure to talk to someone who knows so much. He told me things I didn't know that will be useful when I bring babies."

"But what about you, Ma? What about our baby?"

Ma smiled at Hannah's impatience. "So long as he's just across the street and willing, it seems sensible to have him," she said. "I know your Pa would think the same."

Now she felt everything would be all right with Ma, Hannah enjoyed having the dragoons in town more and more.

Young friends of the lieutenants took to stopping by the barn when they had free time. They treated Hannah and Rachel like grown young ladies and were kind and obliging to Ma. Sometimes if they came on horses, they gave the younger children rides. Lieutenant Smith let Hannah ride Dandy alone back by the barn, and O'Malley let Rachel ride Dolly.

Smith and O'Malley made themselves so much a part of the family that soon Ma took to setting places for them at supper. That often made three extra because Rachel developed the habit of coming to bring a present from the Isaacs' garden or to borrow something just as they were about to sit down and Ma would invite her to stay. Rachel seemed to have forgotten she'd staked claim to a sergeant, and if she ever gave another thought to helping drive cattle to Peekskill, Hannah didn't hear about it.

It was good to have men at table again. For seven months the pastor had been their only man guest, and he was too sober-minded for young people to enjoy. Now there was joking like when Pa was home and man talk that wasn't all about duty. With more work in the house and barn, the days seemed to fly by, but on the other hand it had become so natural to have the dragoons around that it seemed to Hannah they'd been in Bedford forever. One evening at supper it was a surprise to be reminded that it had been less than a week.

Hannah had been listening to Lieutenant O'Malley joking with Andrew and Liddy and managing to flirt with Rachel at the same time when her attention was caught by a snatch of conversation between her mother and Lieutenant Smith. He was telling about something that had happened at New Haven in Connecticut. A burning it was, by redcoats who had come up from New York City in ships. Hannah didn't know anyone in New Haven, and it was too far from Bedford for her to be much interested. But then Smith said, "They landed on the fifth," and Ma replied, "Two days is fast for news to travel."

This did interest her. It meant it was only the seventh of July. Four whole days to wait for the review to which they were all looking forward. Lieutenant O'Malley had told them it wasn't going to be like the parades held every day on the parade ground to call the roll and make inspection. No, this was something different. The cows were to be kept off the Common, and the review would be held there so anyone who wanted could watch. He said the dragoons would show what their horses could do. They'd ride them in different formations, sometimes at a walk, sometimes at a trot, and sometimes at a gallop. They would ride in fours, wheeling at the corners of the Common. They would file off singly. They would pivot to make one straight line. Hannah couldn't remember all the things O'Malley told them, but ninety horses galloping neck to neck in one line right across the Common with manes and tails flying and trumpets sounding orders would surely be something fine to write Pa about, next time she found some way to send a letter.

The review was to be at noon. Hannah and Liddy would wear their good dresses. Rachel had a special dress of fine white muslin embroidered with green sprigs and tiny red roses that Mrs. Isaacs had made over from one of her own. Hannah looked across the table at Rachel, thinking how becoming it would be with her dark eyes and hair. Next to Rachel, Lieutenant O'Malley was leaning down to Liddy on his other side. His blue eyes were twinkling as he asked, "Sweetheart, did I ever tell you about the goat I had in Ireland when I was your age?"

"No. Oh, please tell me. Please." Liddy adored O'Malley and was flattered by his attention.

"Well, he had no nose." The lieutenant stopped as though that were the end of the story.

For a minute Liddy just looked at him and then Hannah and Rachel both saw the question forming in her eyes.

"If he had no nose, how did—?"

"Stop, Liddy! Don't ask him. Don't!" Rachel screeched. "It's a trap!"

"Oh, now, Miss Rachel, why would a lovely young lady like yourself be wanting to spoil the little joke of a poor soldier like me and him so far away from his home?" O'Malley put on such an exaggeratedly woeful face that everyone laughed except Liddy, who threw her arms around his neck to comfort him.

"Tell me. I want to know. I do," she insisted. "If he had no nose, how did he smell?"

O'Malley rumpled her hair. "Well, then, sweetheart, the truth is he smelled terrible."

When the laughter was done, Ma asked Hannah to

clear the table and fetch the pie she'd set to cool in the shed. It was beyond the borning room, and as she passed it, Hannah looked in approvingly. She'd scrubbed it, floor, windows and all, just last week. The doctor for the regiment wouldn't have any complaints about its not being clean.

When she set the pie in front of Ma, Lieutenant O'Malley was asking a riddle.

"From whence I come, 'tis hard to tell, but this I'm sure is known full well. That with the poor I always stay, and am what misers give away."

"An empty stomach?" Andrew guessed. "Poor people are hungry."

"Stupid," Elijah jeered. "Misers don't give their stomachs away! How could they?"

But he couldn't guess either, so finally O'Malley told them. "The answer is *nothing*," he said. "Shall I ask another?"

On Hannah's side of the table, Lieutenant Smith was talking about Pa. "Has he requested parole?" he asked. "Sometimes they let paroled men home to visit."

"A parole was offered," Ma replied, "but my husband refused it. He wasn't willing to give his word not to fight against the British again."

"I heard his colonel was paroled and he's out fighting with his regiment right now."

"And I think the worse of him for breaking his word," Ma said firmly. "We will wait for an exchange and pray it may come soon."

Hannah wondered if she could ever be as brave as Ma. If she had a baby coming, she knew she'd want its father home on any terms.

The evening before the review there were only five at the table. At the last minute the lieutenants sent word they would be with Colonel Moylan at headquarters, and Rachel, too, was absent. After supper Hannah washed the dishes, while her mother set a board across two chairs and started ironing. Glancing over at her, Hannah noticed her face looked tired. Then, with a quick little pang, she noticed something else. The big hump under Ma's apron was much lower down. That meant the baby was getting ready to come soon. Maybe tomorrow.

Not tomorrow, Hannah thought with dismay. She wanted the baby as much as Ma did but not tomorrow! At least not until after the review. When the baby started coming, she'd be needed at home, and she just couldn't bear to miss the review!

"Are you feeling all right, Ma?" she asked, worrying. "Let me finish the ironing—I've done with the dishes."

Ma smiled and shook her head. "No, thank you, Hannah. I'll finish up, but then I think I'll go to bed. I do feel tired."

After Ma had gone upstairs, Rachel came over and walked down to the barn with Hannah to watch her do late-evening chores. Hannah was still worrying about maybe having to miss the review, but before she could even mention it, Rachel said, "I hope Jacob will be home in time tomorrow."

"Jacob?" It had been almost a week since she'd seen him, Hannah suddenly realized.

"Yes, Jacob." Rachel laughed. "Don't say you haven't missed him! Well, it's no harm telling now that he and Papa started to Peekskill four days ago with a drove of cattle. The ones Papa had penned up on a farm north of here."

"But, Rachel, I thought you wanted to go with them, and you never said one word!"

"Well, I changed my mind. The dragoons are fun. Especially Lieutenant O'Malley."

While Hannah was forking down hay from the loft, Rachel gave each of the horses a little grain and made sure they had plenty of water. Dolly was Rachel's favorite because she belonged to O'Malley, so she lingered a minute in her stall, stroking her velvet nose.

Then she turned to Hannah. "I've decided Dolly is going to be the best-groomed horse of them all tomorrow, and I'm going to start on her right now," she said.

"Well, then I'll work on Dandy," Hannah replied. "I don't want his nose out of joint." Of course the lieutenants would groom again in the morning, but an hour with brush and polish now would bring an extra shine to the horses' coats and to their saddles and bridles.

It was getting late when the girls finished and stood back to admire their work. "They surely do look fine." Rachel sighed with satisfaction. "I can hardly wait for tomorrow."

When she went upstairs, Hannah stopped and peeked into her mother's room. Ma was lying asleep on her back in the big double bed that seemed too big without Pa. She looked rested and comfortable. If only—if only she'd hold onto the baby until after the review tomorrow!

CHAPTER 7

The rooster next door crowed, waking Hannah. The room was still dark, but through the windows the sky showed pale gray. Soon it would be light indoors as well as out and time to get up. Hannah waited. In a moment she should hear the notes of reveille floating up from the camp by the river. In the quiet of early morning she always listened for reveille to start her day as well as that of the dragoons.

Old Fred, the Mills' rooster, added his voice to the voice of the cock next door. All up and down the street others joined in. Inside the room, the chair and washstand took on shape. Hannah waited until she could distinguish the blue of Liddy's everyday dress and the brown of her own among the clothes hanging on pegs under the high shelf near the door. She must have slept right through reveille.

Dressing quickly, Hannah stole downstairs, shoes in hand, so as not to disturb her mother. The longer Ma slept, the better. If she didn't move around too much, maybe the baby would stay quiet, too, and not start coming until after the review.

Hannah got some kindling and small split logs from the wood box in the shed and laid them on last night's embers, so there'd be a fire ready for Ma to make breakfast. There was still no sound above stairs when she went out through the shed door, taking a clean shining milk pail off its peg on her way. The sun wasn't up yet, and heavy mist lay on the back field and meadows clear to the river. It was like an enchanted lake and hid the tents of the camp as completely as though they were actually submerged. A soft breeze stirred in the leaves of the lilac by the back doorstep. Hannah drew a deep breath of fresh morning air. It was going to be a fine day.

After running down to the barn, she opened both the big doors to let in the light and the morning coolness. Old Fred crowed, the hens cackled, and Magnolia mooed, but there were no welcoming whinnies from Dandy and Dolly. The horse stalls were empty and, by the looks of them, had been empty most of the night. Puzzled and a little worried, Hannah set about morning chores. First she let the chickens out to hunt insects in the dewy grass and started collecting eggs.

Colonel Moylan must have chosen the lieutenants for some unexpected duty when they were at headquarters last night, she decided. That they were late in returning was nothing to worry about except the horses might not be as fresh as they should be for the review. If Dolly and Dandy didn't show off to the same advantage as the other horses, she didn't believe either she or Rachel would ever forgive Moylan.

Six eggs, seven, ten, eleven. Enough to spare some for the Indian pudding Lieutenant Smith liked so much. Setting the egg basket on a shelf, Hannah cleaned Magnolia's stall and put feed in the box in front of her. Then she washed the cow's udder and drew up the milking stool.

A double stream of milk came down into the pail, one stream a little after the other as her hands worked in steady rhythm. The streams pinged on the empty bottom of the pail, then as it began to fill, they hissed and foamed. It wasn't a loud sound but, since she was right on top of it, loud enough to shut out the sound of footsteps.

"Hannah!" She hadn't heard Andrew come into the barn and at first was only annoyed by the loudness of his voice. A less placid cow might hold back her milk or kick over the pail when startled like that. Even Magnolia shifted her weight and switched her tail into Hannah's face.

"Hannah! Ma says to let Magnolia out quick!"

"But I haven't finished milking."

"That doesn't matter. I'm to take her to the woods right away!"

"Andrew, you must have heard Ma wrong. Go back and ask her what she really said."

"No, Hannah! She did say the woods and right away." Andrew was shouting with frustration, and then he burst into tears. "Oh, Hannah, something terrible is happening. I don't know what, but it's happening."

Hannah jumped up and put a comforting arm around him, but Andrew shook it off. "Let me go," he bawled. "Ma says I've got to take Magnolia, and Liddy, too."

"Liddy?" Thoroughly alarmed now, Hannah watched Andrew release Magnolia's head from the stanchion and tie a rope to her halter. She didn't even protest when the milk pail turned over on the floor. "Wait, Andrew," she begged, but he ran out the door, dragging Magnolia behind him to where Liddy waited, wide-eyed with fright.

For a minute Hannah stood there rooted, staring after the two small figures trudging off toward the woods. Then she sped to the house.

"Ma, oh, Ma," she cried. "What is it?"

Ma was standing on the stoop with her back to the front door, facing toward the crossroads. Her face was pale, but she looked composed.

"British and Hessians, they say. And De Lancey's riffraff."

"Where, Ma? Where? I don't see them." Then Hannah heard a shout.

"They must be nearly here," Ma told her in an even quiet voice. "A man rode by a couple of minutes ago to give us warning."

"But, Ma, they can't hurt us. Moylan won't let them," Hannah exclaimed confidently. "It won't take the dragoons long to saddle and mount. The dragoons will send them flying."

"No," Ma said. "The dragoons aren't here. They were ordered to Norwalk on the Sound last night. The lieutenants told me when they came for their horses."

"They shouldn't have left us. They shouldn't!" Hannah cried. "Moylan said they were here to protect Bedford."

"Hush," Ma said, "and listen."

In front of almost every house, people were gathered. Most, like Ma, were trying to listen. But some of the women were crying and running back and forth, bringing things out of the houses. East of the Common the Seeleys were frantically loading a farm wagon. Hannah saw beds and bedding being piled on top of lanterns and earthenware. A trunk was hoisted on top of a spinning wheel and an iron pot on a wall clock. The son, Elijah's age, led a cow from the barn and tied it at the back of the wagon. Hannah tried to stay quiet the way Ma wanted, but the panic of the family across the way was catching. She felt an answering panic rising up in her, and when the old grandfather on the front seat whipped up the team and they came careening past, she couldn't contain it any longer.

"Ma, don't just stand there!" she burst out. "Do something. Tell me what to do. Should I bring things from the house? What about the militia? Where's Elijah?"

"Hush," Ma said again, and then she added, "We don't know yet that the soldiers are coming through the village. They may be looking for Moylan or they may be headed for Norwalk and go right past on the upper road."

"But if they do come here, Ma? What'll we do?"

"Just stay calm, Hannah. If they're hoping to surprise Moylan, they won't stay long when they find he's gone. The militia's gone, too, and they won't harm women and children and old folks unless they're provoked. But they might loot some. That's why I sent Magnolia off."

It wasn't easy to stay calm. Especially when Elijah came running toward them across the Common.

"They're coming this way, Ma," he yelled and when he reached the house and caught his breath, he went on, "They're stopping at houses and asking for Moylan. There's hundreds—"

"All right, Elijah," Ma said. "Now remember, Moylan left last night. Tell them that if they ask and no matter what anyone says, you be polite."

While Ma was still speaking, Hannah saw the first of the enemy party. It halted outside the house Moylan had used as headquarters. Then it came on, followed by the whole body. Elijah had been right. There were hundreds. Green coats, red coats, and some in makeshift uniforms. So many that the dragoons would have been outnumbered four to one at least. They swept by at a gallop headed for the camp by the river. Only of course it wasn't there now. Except for the mist, they'd have known.

It took several minutes for all of them to pass. When the last had gone by, Hannah let out the breath she'd been holding so long she felt dizzy.

"What do we do now, Ma?" she asked.

"Get breakfast," her mother replied.

"Shall I go for Andrew and Liddy?"

"Not yet." Ma went inside, and Hannah followed her.

"I saw Tamar's uncle," she told her mother.

"I saw him, too," Ma said. "He was with De Lancey's Refugees. I should think Roger Halstead would be ashamed to show his face with them in Bedford."

"Ma, when they don't find Moylan—are you sure they will just go away?"

"No, Hannah, I'm not but there'd be no—" Suddenly Ma caught onto the back of a chair for support, and her face twisted. The next moment she was herself again.

"You all right, Ma?" Hannah cried out in alarm. "Is it the baby? Is it coming? Now?"

"Yes," her mother replied calmly. "It started awhile back."

"You want Elijah to go for the doctor right away?" Hannah asked before she remembered. There was no doctor in Bedford now.

"Send him for Mrs. Woolsey," Ma told her.

"Not Mrs. Woolsey! No, Ma, please!" Hannah protested.

"Do as you're told, Hannah," her mother said sharply. When Ma spoke like that, it was no use to argue.

After Elijah left, Hannah went back into the house. Ma had taken Pa's letters from the box on the mantelshelf and was stuffing them down the front of her dress. At first she looked as though she were sorry Hannah had caught her at it, but then she smiled. For a moment she looked almost like a girl. "It will be next best to having your Pa here himself," she said. "I've never had a baby come without him here before."

Hannah threw her arms around her mother, but she couldn't think of a single comforting thing to say. Ma stroked her hair gently. "Don't be upset for me, honey. Maybe it's lucky Pa isn't here. When the soldiers see for themselves that the campsite's empty, they may act ugly, and your pa has a hasty temper."

Then Hannah knew. In spite of not acting scared, Ma was expecting trouble. Maybe inside she'd been scared of it all along. If Ma was scared— To keep from thinking about that, Hannah busied herself getting things ready for the birthing. She fetched more water from the well and put another kettle on the crane to boil. She got ready a basin and soap and cloths. But all the time she was listening. She couldn't help it. Her eardrums felt stretched from listening.

Then it began. A low angry rumble that sounded like thunder in the distance. Coming from the direction of the campsite. Growing louder and angrier. The soldiers were heading back toward the village.

Down the street a woman screamed. The scream was drowned in an ugly roar. Hannah shivered. It was like a hundred bulls all bellowing at the same time. At first there were no words to it that she could make out. Suddenly she stiffened. There was a word. It sounded like "BURN." She heard it again and again. BURN, BURN, BURN. She was sure of it now. The voices rose in wild, excited shouts.

"Oh, Ma!" Hannah ran to her mother, clutching at her. "They are going to burn. What'll we do?"

"Pray," Ma said. "Pray that God will change their hearts." Holding onto the seat of a chair, Ma got awkwardly down on her knees. Hannah knelt beside her, but she couldn't keep her mind on praying.

The sound of rioting was sweeping toward them. "Burn them out! Burn the rebels out!"

Horses neighed; men shouted; women screamed. Then right outside their own house pebbles clattered against the stoop as horses came to a sudden stop. Spurs clinked as men dismounted. There was a burst of laughter and a piece of flaming wood came hurtling through the door onto the braided rug.

Hannah looked at it in horror and then at her mother. But Ma was gripping the seat of the chair so hard her knuckles were white. Her eyes were closed, and her lips drawn tight in pain. Right now Ma couldn't help, and there wasn't even a moment to wait for the pain to pass. The rug already smelled of singeing wool. Hannah grasped the torch by the end and flung it back out the door. It landed on the stoop, and she ran out and kicked it onto the walk.

All up and down the street as far as she could see, men were gathered making ready to burn. The ones standing in front of their house were talking excitedly in a strange thick tongue. Behind them an officer sat aloof on a handsome black steed.

"Stop, oh, please stop!" she cried desperately. "My mother's inside. She's having a baby. It's started coming."

The men didn't seem to understand. They were crowding closer, shouting and brandishing torches.

"Please, please don't burn us!" Hannah raised her voice against theirs, even though she knew it was useless. These men must be the Hessians she'd heard about. They spoke only German.

The officer gave a command in the same language, and the men halted with arms still upraised.

"Are you telling the truth, miss?" he asked in English. "Is your mother really in labor, or is this just a story to turn us from our duty?"

"It's true—oh, it's true!" Hannah cried.

"Well, then," the officer said, "you shall see we Hessians are not inhumane." Hannah was babbling her thanks when he cut her short. "We shall delay a little so you may get your mother out of the house and what she will need for her comfort."

Hannah stared at him openmouthed. He was going to burn the house down after all.

"We will wait here in the street," he added. "Please accept our kind wishes to your mother for a fine healthy child."

Without a word Hannah turned away from him and ran back into the house. Her mother was still on her knees, but Hannah could tell by her face that the pain had gone.

"Oh, Ma," she sobbed, "I hoped our prayers had been answered. I hoped they were going to spare our house."

Ma struggled clumsily to her feet, still holding onto the chair. "I heard," she said, "and our prayers were answered. God gave you courage to say what you did, and He saw to it the officer listened. Even a little time is a blessing, so stop crying and pour water on the rug."

It was as if Ma had been away and now was back. Smoke was coming in from the street, but Ma was there beside her to tell her what to do. They carried things through the shed and set them outside on the grass. Ma decided what to take, but Hannah did the running up and downstairs because Ma was slow, and she lifted the real heavy things like kettles and Pa's box of carpenter's tools. Then Ma chose the place that would be safest when the Hessians burned them. It was by the well, halfway between the house and the barn. Hannah dragged out the mattress from the borning room for Ma to rest on while she carried the things piled by the shed door down to her.

Every time Hannah ran between the house and the well she saw more of the village blazing. The Baylors' house on one side and the Slawsons' on the other were both in flames. The smoke was so thick that it choked her, and Ma was coughing, too. When Hannah had carried down all the things that were piled outside the shed, she ran back into the house. Ma's sewing basket had made her think of the christening dress Mrs. Isaacs had made for the baby. She took it, still folded in its clean paper, out of the chest by Ma's bed.

Coming downstairs again, she met the Hessian officer.

"You have had time enough," he said. "We can wait no longer."

Then the soldiers ran in from the street, carrying their torches of burning wood. They overran the yard, laughing and shouting at one another as they made a sport of setting fires. In minutes the house and barn and outbuildings were crackling and blazing. With a lewd gesture one of the soldiers set fire to the two-hole necessary house. But none of them came near the well.

Hannah sat beside Ma on the mattress. Everything that had been home all her life was going. Behind the flames licking out from the windows of the house were things she'd never see again. Ma's spinning wheel and loom, the tall clock that had been a wedding present, the pine cupboard, and the long table where they gathered to eat and listen to Ma read the Bible. It was like losing friends. Hannah looked at Ma. Her eyes were closed, lips moving. She was praying.

There was a sound like a clap of thunder. Smoke poured from a gap in the roof and then the roof fell in and disappeared. Sparks landed near the mattress and the pile of things they'd saved. Hannah got up and doused the sparks with water from the well and then took some to Ma to drink. They could scarcely stand the heat that enveloped them. It came from their buildings and the Slawsons' and the Baylors'. Hannah could see their neighbors standing, doing nothing except keeping their children close. No one was trying to put out flames. There was no use.

The Hessians had gone back to the street. They were waiting there with other soldiers, ready to reset any fires that might be extinguished.

After a while Ma said, "They're leaving," and Hannah paused, bucket still in hand, to see them go. They rode down the Street toward White Plains, driving a

bunch of cattle. Dust followed them, and then that, too, was gone.

Then Ma called her. "The baby's coming faster than I thought. I have to tell you what to do if Mrs. Woolsey doesn't get here."

Hannah had seen farm animals and kittens born, and Ma tried to make this sound as easy. "Just take the baby when it comes out and lay it on the mattress beside me. Be careful not to break the cord. I'll attend to that myself when I've rested a little."

When the next pain came, Hannah could tell it was different. Ma didn't just stay still while the hurt lasted. She was straining against it. "Should be soon now," she gasped. "The head will come first."

"I know, Ma," Hannah said. "I've heard." But she hadn't known how bad the pains would be before that happened. Ma clenched her teeth and tried not to cry out, but she couldn't hide the suffering. It was almost more than Hannah could bear.

"I didn't know it hurt so much—oh, Ma, I didn't know."

"It's a good hurt," Ma said when that pain had passed. "Once the baby's here, I won't remember it."

The pains came closer and closer together until there was hardly any time between them at all. And with each, Ma strained. Hannah felt herself straining, too, as though that would help.

When the sun was halfway to noon, Ma stopped working to bring the baby. She lay, still and exhausted, except when convulsed with pain. "It's no use, Hannah," she said. "God grant Elijah has found Mrs. Woolsey and she comes soon."

Hannah had hoped the baby would be lying safe in Ma's arms before Mrs. Woolsey had a chance to touch it or touch Ma. But now all she, too, wanted was for the old midwife to come quick. When at last she saw her witchlike figure hobbling toward them from the Street, she ran to her, sobbing with relief.

Mrs. Woolsey spoke to Ma and then stooped and laid gentle hands on her stomach.

"It's lying wrong, but it won't be hard to straighten," she said.

Then she spoke to Hannah. "Go up by your Ma's head, ducky, and let her hang onto you."

Before Hannah knew what was happening, Mrs. Woolsey had her hand and wrist right inside Ma. Ma cried out just once. With the next pain the baby came. "Little girl," Mrs. Woolsey said.

CHAPTER 8

"*Dear Pa,*" *Hannah began her letter.* "*The baby is a girl. She got born three days ago. She's not* pretty yet, but Ma says she will be."

She stopped there and thought, leaning against the coping of the well. What should she say next? How could she tell Pa that everything was burned, so it wouldn't seem as bad as it was? Ma would know the right words, but there wasn't time to go ask her because Major Tallmadge might want his writing things back any minute. He was on his way to the Hudson and would send her letter from there if it was finished before he was ready to leave. She'd just have to do the best she could by herself.

"We are living up by Indian Hill now," she wrote, and then crossed that out with three broad lines. She'd have to tell about Bedford first or Pa would think they had lost their senses to move away from home. Besides, putting off the bad part wouldn't help any. She'd best get it over with.

"Pa, you have to know. Bedford got burned. Everything from the meetinghouse to south of the Common is gone. Except for the Halsteads' house. It was British and Tory Refugees and Hessians that did the burning. Norwalk was burned the same day by redcoats coming down from New Haven. That's why the dragoons weren't here, or the militia."

A fat bluegreen fly lit on her arm. She brushed it off with a grimace of disgust. Most likely it had been feasting on some burned animal that wasn't buried yet. There were a lot of dead things still unburied in the village. They smelled bad, and so did the charred beams that had fallen into cellars and still smoldered there. All that was left standing were smoke-blackened chimneys, pointing like dirty fingers toward the clean blue sky. Except for one or two families where the men were home, no one had started to clear their yards of debris. There was such a feeling of desolation in the ruined village that Hannah dreaded coming back to it for things they needed.

It was lucky though, that Ma had sent her down for vegetables and eggs. If she hadn't come, she'd have missed seeing Major Tallmadge, and it might have been weeks before Pa would have known about the baby. It wasn't easy to send letters from Bedford.

She glanced toward the street where Major Tallmadge, standing beside his horse, was talking with Ezra Hunter. Hannah didn't know the sharp-faced man except by sight, but she'd seen him with Mr. Halstead once or twice. Some claimed he gave information to the British. It probably wasn't true, but she wondered if Major Tallmadge knew what was being said. Perhaps she'd ask when she gave him Pa's letter. She went back to writing it.

"Some families are staying with folks outside the village until things get cleared up. Some are living in shelters against the cliffs at the bottom of Indian Hill. We have a real nice shelter. At the back it's a shallow cave with a rock sticking out over it like the roof of a porch. The front is built of saplings that Jacob Isaacs and Elijah cut down. It's lucky we saved your tools. We saved a lot of other things, too. Enough to share with the Isaacs' until they can buy new. They lost everything except the horses Mr. Isaacs and Jacob were using to drive cattle to Peekskill."

What else should she tell Pa so he wouldn't worry about them? She brushed at another fly that was trying to settle on her and started writing again.

"We are as comfortable as can be, Pa. We have blankets and quilts and some clothes and things to cook with. We have a place to cook, too, right outside the shelter. It's made of three big stones Elijah and Jacob pushed together. We have plenty of food. Magnolia didn't get taken or burned, so we have milk. We tether her near us at night and keep her milk cool in the stream by the road. The chickens are laying fine in the grass outside where the barn was. Our vegetables didn't get tramped on, and the raspberries are ripe enough to eat."

Hannah had made her writing small, but even so there wasn't much room left on the paper Major Tallmadge had given her, and she still had to explain about the money she was going to send with the letter.

"The money is for you to buy something, if it's enough. It's my share of what the dragoons paid for taking care of their horses. They forgot to pay, but after the battle at Norwalk they remembered and sent it back by Major Tallmadge. He was at Norwalk, too."

It was four nights since Moylan's dragoons had gone to Norwalk, leaving Bedford to be burned by the enemy. Ma said it wasn't Moylan's fault, but Hannah couldn't accept that. She kept remembering that wonderful, exciting morning when he'd marched into Bedford, promising to defend it and its people. Well, he hadn't. He wasn't even coming back. When he gave her the money, Major Tallmadge told her Moylan's regiment was to remain in Connecticut. Probably she'd never see the lieutenants again, Hannah thought with a pang. She felt ashamed of its mattering, but it did. They'd all had such fun the week the lieutenants were part of the family.

Hannah took another look toward the street. The major had his foot in the stirrup. She had better finish her letter.

"Take care of yourself, Pa, and don't fret about us. We are all doing fine. The baby is going to be christened next Sunday after morning meeting. It will be outdoors by the burying ground because that's all there is left of Bedford. Not counting the Halsteads' house. Ma said you settled on Amy if it was a girl. She has a beautiful christening dress we saved. Mrs. Isaacs made it."

At the bottom Hannah wrote, "Your loving and obedient daughter," and signed her name.

Then she read the letter over. She hadn't said anything Ma wouldn't have wanted. She hadn't told how the baby cried all the time or that Ma had lost her appetite except for the tea made from herbs Mrs. Woolsey brought. She hadn't said Tabby, the cat, was missing since the fire and Liddy was grieving for her. And she'd only said the good things about Elijah. About how he'd worked with Jacob on the shelter and fireplace. She hadn't told how he'd sassed one of the soldiers the day of the burning and been tied to a tree in back of the Halsteads' house.

Ezra Hunter had left while Hannah wasn't noticing, and now Tallmadge was turning his horse into the yard. She went to meet him.

"I'd be glad if you could send this money along with the letter," she said, handing him back two of the four dollars he had given her from the lieutenants.

"I will if you want me to," Tallmadge replied, "but won't you need it? When he learns about the fire, I think your father would rather you kept it."

"No," Hannah said. "I told him we have everything we need. Will it be enough, though, for Pa to buy anything? I've heard the British don't like paper money."

Major Tallmadge laughed. It was the first laugh Hannah had heard in three days, and it was stifled almost immediately. "That is putting it mildly, Hannah. But two Continental dollars could buy an extra loaf of bread or a little more time exercising in the prison yard from a guard in a good humor."

He returned his pen and ink flask to his saddlebag and put Hannah's letter and the money in an inside pocket of his jacket.

"Sir—" She hesitated.

"Yes, Hannah?"

"Most likely it isn't true. And maybe you know anyway, but some say Mr. Hunter spies for the British."

"I do know, Hannah, but thank you."

That's all he said. Not whether he thought it was true or not. Feeling that maybe she'd spoken out of place, Hannah was a little uncomfortable as she watched the major ride north toward the crossroads. When she could no longer see him, she gathered as many eggs as she could find and some carrots. Then she drew some water from the well for the chickens and started back toward Indian Hill.

"Hannah!" The voice was Tamar's. Hannah didn't stop or turn around, but Tamar caught up with her.

"Hannah, please stop walking and listen." The voice trembled a little. "My mother sent me to ask how your mother is doing and to say, if she wants, you are all welcome to stay at our house while the baby's so little."

Hannah did turn then. Tamar's dress was clean, and her blond hair brushed shiny. Unconsciously Hannah's hand went up to her own hair. It felt sticky, and her dress was as dirty as Mrs. Woolsey's old skirt. Well, right now she didn't care.

"At your house?" All the scorn she felt went into the words. "At the only house in Bedford that wasn't burned, on account of your uncle being with the Refugees?"

"Oh, Hannah!" Tamar looked as though Hannah had slapped her. "Don't hold that against us. I'd rather our house had burned, too. Can't you understand?"

"No."

For a moment neither girl said anything more. Then Tamar straightened her shoulders and said with dignity, "I've asked what my mother sent me to ask. That's all."

"I'll tell Ma," Hannah replied. She felt like adding, "Don't be expecting us, though," but she didn't. That was for Ma to say.

Ma was asleep inside the shelter when Hannah got back to Indian Hill, and little Amy was crying. She took the baby outside and rocked her in her arms so Ma wouldn't wake. Amy was cute, but she smelled sour. She'd spit up on her muslin shirt. Andrew and Liddy were playing quietly with sticks outside, building a small house for a furry brown and black caterpillar.

"It's a kind of kitty," Andrew said. Liddy nodded, but she wasn't convinced or consoled for the loss of Tabby.

When the caterpillar was safely installed, Andrew lifted serious eyes to Hannah's.

"Hannah, why does Amy spit up her food?"

"I guess all babies do," Hannah replied.

"Did I?" Liddy looked up, interested.

"Probably. I can't remember."

"Ben doesn't," Andrew stated authoritatively. "Not all the time anyway. Aaron says just once in a while."

"Well, Amy will stop when she's Ben's age," Hannah assured him, but she really wasn't sure, and she didn't want to ask Ma. She didn't want Andrew or Liddy asking either. She wished she could remember more clearly how it had been when Liddy was born. Had Ma been strong again sooner then, or was she remembering wrong?

Hannah forgot to keep rocking Amy, and the baby let out a wail. Ma woke and took her into the shelter to feed.

While Amy was nursing, Hannah told her mother about meeting Major Tallmadge and getting the money and about writing to Pa.

Ma smiled over the dark fuzz on the top of the baby's head. "I'm glad you sent Pa some of the money," she said. "I wish you had sent it all. Did you tell him we are comfortable? And how pretty Amy is?"

"Yes, I did, Ma. At least I said Amy would be." She dug in her pocket and brought out the bills. "Shall I put the money somewhere for you, Ma?"

Her mother looked around the shelter. The only piece of furniture they'd saved was a small table Pa had made the week before he went off with his militia company and was captured. On it was Ma's sewing basket and the Bible.

"Put it in the basket, Hannah," Ma said. "In my needle case."

There was something else Hannah had to tell. "Ma, I met Tamar on the way back. She said we are welcome to stay at their house for a while. Mrs. Halstead sent her to say so."

Amy was fussing, and Ma changed her to the other breast. "That was kind of Mrs. Halstead."

"You're not going to say yes, are you, Ma?" Hannah asked in sudden alarm.

Her mother shook her head. "No, Hannah, we are comfortable here, but you must go and give Mrs. Halstead my thanks."

"No, Ma, I can't. I just can't!" Hannah protested. "I don't ever want to go in that house or speak to Tamar again."

Ma's face took on her "do-as-I-tell-you" look, and Hannah wondered what she would do if Ma really said it. Then Ma's expression changed, and she gave a tired sigh. "All right, Hannah," she said. "I won't ask it. Elijah is off somewhere. When he comes back, I'll send him."

CHAPTER 9

*In the afternoon Hannah and Rachel climbed to the top of Indian Hill for blueberries. It seemed a hun-*dred years since they'd come there looking for Moylan the day Pound Ridge was raided.

"Do you think Bedford will ever be the same again?" Rachel asked, putting half a handful of berries into her basket and the other half into her mouth. "I want it to be."

"So do I," Hannah replied.

"Papa is going to rebuild our house just the way it was," Rachel said. "Won't your father, too, when he gets back?"

"I guess so." But until Pa got exchanged, there was no sense in thinking about their own rebuilding, and exchange didn't seem any nearer. The taking of British prisoners at Pound Ridge wouldn't help Pa a bit because Tarleton had proposed a private exchange of the men captured there.

Hannah dropped a few berries into her own basket. She didn't want to talk about Pa, even to Rachel. To get the conversation away from him, she said, "Andrew and Liddy want to live in a shelter forever. They pretend they're Indians most of the time."

"Well, it is nice for the summer," Rachel agreed. "I hope Papa doesn't find a place on a farm for Mama and Ben and me and Aaron to board. I'd rather stay right here with him and Jacob until our house is up again."

"Oh, Rachel, I didn't know he was looking!" Hannah cried in dismay. "Why didn't you tell me? If you go away, I'll be so lonesome I'll just about die."

"Well, he hasn't really started looking yet, and he didn't say anything about it till this morning. Then he said we should have a place where Mama and I can spin and weave." Rachel made a face. "And he said it would be better for Ben on account of it's hard to keep him clean without a real place to wash clothes. But he's promised that even if he finds a place, we can stay here until after Amy's christening."

"I guess it would be better for Amy to live inside, too, like Ben," Hannah said. "But we can't afford boarding." She hesitated and then went on. "We had a chance to live in a house, though. The Halsteads'! Can you see us doing that, Rachel?"

"No, I can't. I wouldn't either," Rachel replied. "But I'm sorry for Tamar. Imagine being the only girl in Bedford whose house wasn't burned."

"She said she'd rather it had burned." Hannah snorted. "As if I'd believe that."

"Well, I do," Rachel said. "I told her so."

"You spoke to her!" Hannah exclaimed. "When?"

"This morning. She felt awful. What happened wasn't her fault. You had no need to say what you did."

Hannah moved to another clump of bushes. If Rachel wanted to stand up for Tamar, she was welcome to, but she needn't expect her to feel sorry for any Halstead.

For a while they picked in separate places, and then Rachel said, "I have enough. I'm going back down."

A minute or so later Hannah followed. At the bottom of the path the Isaacs' shelter was the first she passed. Andrew and Liddy were there with Aaron. If Rachel had been in sight, Hannah would have stopped and said something friendly to make things right between them again. But she wasn't, so Hannah went on.

The road looked strange with temporary shelters huddled against the cliffs. The Baylors had simply cut saplings and rested the ends against the rock wall to make a rough lean-to. The Slawsons had used standing trees for corner posts and nailed saplings crossways between them. All the shelters were crude, but children were playing happily around them, and women were chatting with neighbors at their outside fireplaces. The Browns were going to have rabbit stew for supper, Hannah noted with interest. Well, their own supper was going to be good, too. Mr. Isaacs had given them some cornmeal he'd bought from a farmer, and they were having johnnycake made with blueberries and trout that Elijah had caught.

When Hannah got back to the Mills' shelter, Mrs. Isaacs was there with little Ben. She had put him down on a blanket and was holding Amy instead. Amy was crying as usual, and beside the older baby, she looked even punier than Hannah had thought.

"Let me nurse Amy this once, Elizabeth," Mrs. Isaacs suggested. "I have more than enough milk for Ben, and perhaps you aren't giving her all she needs."

At first Ma didn't want to, but then she agreed and watched with a yearning anxious look while Amy nursed hungrily.

"I never had a baby I couldn't satisfy before," she said when Mrs. Isaacs gave Amy back to her. "I'm grateful to you, Esther."

Mrs. Isaacs smiled. "It's a small return for all that good milk of Magnolia's you share with us. I'll nurse her again tomorrow if you'll let me."

The next day Mrs. Isaacs nursed Amy twice. The baby slept soundly after each feeding, and Ma should have rested, too. Only she didn't. She boiled clothes in the big iron kettle and spread them out on bushes to dry in the hot sun. Her face was flushed, and her eyes were very bright. Then she began to shiver and asked Hannah to fetch her shawl from inside the shelter.

Mrs. Baylor stopped by to visit, and she glanced sharply at Ma.

"You look feverish," she said. "I'll bring you some salts of wormwood. It's lucky I saved our box of remedies."

Hannah's heart skipped a beat, but Ma said no, there was nothing wrong except a sudden draft right after the heat from the boiling kettle.

By morning, though, word had spread that Ma was feverish. One after another the women from neighboring shelters came, suggesting remedies. A broth made from the uncleaned entrails of an old hen, a toad boiled with honey and beetles, a bloodletting.

Ma was polite about all the suggestions, but the visits tired her. When Hannah begged her to lie down and rest, she refused.

"Don't worry," she said. "I'll be right as rain in a few days. Just make me some herb tea."

Hannah tried not to worry and to believe every day that Ma was better. And sometimes she did seem better. When Hannah went down to the village for eggs and vegetables, she always told everyone she saw that Ma was doing fine. But on her way back to the shelter her legs would go faster and faster till she was running before she got there, because she was scared that Ma would be worse.

Mrs. Isaacs was giving Amy nearly all her feedings now and keeping Liddy and Andrew with Aaron as much as she could, so Ma could rest quiet when she wanted. Elijah hung around the shelter a lot of the time, just looking at Ma. The way he looked made Hannah nervous. As if he were trying to fix Ma's face in his mind.

Then one night Hannah woke to hear Ma talking. "Yes, Ma?" she said, but Ma wasn't talking to her. She was talking to Grandma Mills, who'd been dead three years. After that she started to talk to Pa. Only it was the Pa of their courting days. Hannah was almost ashamed to listen. She touched Ma to wake her. Ma felt so hot it was if she were burning, and she kept right on talking to Pa. Hannah ran out of the shelter and dipped one of Amy's diaper cloths in a bucket of cool water to put on Ma's head. Elijah was sleeping outside with Andrew and Liddy. Hannah thought of waking him, but she didn't, and a few minutes later Ma stopped talking. For a while Hannah bathed her forehead and then, exhausted, went back to sleep.

Toward morning Ma called to Hannah in her usual voice but low so the others wouldn't waken.

"Put Amy to my breast, Hannah. I'd like to nurse her once more if I can while I talk to you." Then she said, "Hannah, I'm dying. There's no use hoping anything different now. It's the fever. It happens after birthing sometimes. I've seen it often enough to know."

"Don't say that, Ma! Don't say it!" Hannah begged, panic making her voice shrill.

"I have to, Hannah, and you have to listen. So you'll know what to do when I'm gone. Mrs. Isaacs will care for Amy till she's weaned, but you have to see to the others until your pa gets back."

"I won't know how," Hannah sobbed. "Please don't leave us, Ma."

"You know all you need. I've taught you. And Elijah will help if you put it to him right."

"He won't. He never does." Hannah's wail wasn't really on account of Elijah.

"Yes, he will. But even if you have a hard time at first, don't let on. If you do, some will think you're not old enough to manage and try to separate you all into different homes. I don't want that, Hannah, and neither would your pa. You belong together, where you can live according to what Pa and I have taught you is right. Promise me you will stay together."

"Yes, Ma, I promise." Hannah's throat ached so from the big lump in it that she could hardly speak.

"The money—" Ma's voice went suddenly weak.

"It's in the needle case," Hannah reminded.

"No, there's more. It's—" Ma stopped, and when she spoke again, she was a little girl, telling her own ma she was sorry for spilling her milk.

Ma didn't die that day, but fever burned her and chills shook her, and she lived in a world where Hannah couldn't reach her.

Early the next morning Mrs. Isaacs came to nurse Amy. But seeing how Ma was, she took the baby to her own shelter, and Andrew and Liddy, too. "You can come home later on," she promised the frightened children, "just as soon as your mama says so. I'll leave them with Rachel as soon as I've fed Amy," she told Hannah. "Then I will come back and help with your mother."

All day people came to help. It was kind of them, but except for Mrs. Isaacs, Hannah wished they'd go away. They told stories about friends and relatives who'd died of childbed fever. She was glad Ma didn't know what they were saying.

Hannah ran up to the top of Indian Hill to escape the talk when she couldn't bear it any longer, and so she wasn't there when the pastor came. But when she returned, Mrs. Baylor said she'd arranged with him to put the christening off until Ma got better or she died. Mrs. Baylor liked arranging things.

"I hate Amy!" Elijah suddenly burst out. "If Ma dies, it's because of her. And I hate all of you, too. You *want* Ma to die."

When it got close to suppertime, the women left one by one. Then Mrs Woolsey came, bringing more herbs. She brewed them into tea, but Ma was beyond taking more than a swallow, and she wasn't conscious of taking that. Mrs. Woolsey stayed on without being asked, and when Ma died at daybreak, she prepared her body for burial.

Mr. Isaacs and Jacob made a box of pine boards they got at the Slawsons' mill and put Ma in it. With the fever gone and her hair braided neat like a girl's, she looked prettier and younger than she had for a long time. Amy looked almost pretty, too. Mrs. Isaacs had washed her and put on the christening dress. Before the lid was nailed on Ma's coffin, Andrew and Liddy put flowers on her crossed hands. They were dry-eyed because they had no tears left. Elijah was standing silent and apart. Hannah knew he was feeling bad, but he just looked angry.

The procession to the burial ground was slow. Walking behind the coffin, Hannah held Liddy's hand. Elijah and Andrew followed. Mrs. Baylor came next, carrying Amy. As Ma's oldest neighbor, she'd claimed the right to act as the baby's sponsor.

At last they came to the Common and crossed it to the burying ground. There was a big hole among the Mills' graves, and Hannah knew it was for Ma. She could hardly listen to what the pastor was saying. While he went on and on, she kept dreading the moment when they'd put Ma in the ground. Then they did.

As the coffin was lowered into the grave, Liddy clutched at Hannah, hiding her head in the skirts that only partly muffled her howls.

". . . we therefore commit her body . . ." the pastor intoned.

"Hush, Liddy," Hannah whispered.

". . . resurrection to eternal life through our Lord, Jesus Christ. Amen."

It was over, the moment Hannah had feared she couldn't endure. Gently she disentangled Liddy from her skirts.

"She's not really in that hole, Liddy. She's up in heaven with Grandma Mills and the twins."

"I want her here with us," the little girl sobbed.

"So do I, oh, so do I!" The cry almost tore Hannah apart, though it never reached her lips.

Taking a few short steps to a stone where a basin of water rested, the pastor went right on to Amy's baptism with scarcely a pause for breath.

When that, too, was finished, Mrs. Baylor handed the now-screaming baby over to Mrs. Isaacs, who received her in loving arms. Hannah, still holding onto Liddy, stood white-faced and stiff, listening to words of consolation. She wanted to run away from them, to the top of Indian Hill or any other place where she could be alone to weep for Ma the way she needed to.

But it would shame Ma if she did. So she stood there saying, "Thank you, sir," or "It's kind of you, ma'am, we'll be all right," until the very last person had gone.

CHAPTER 10

For three weeks, Elijah hadn't milked Magnolia even once.

"It's not my turn," he'd said when Hannah asked him to, the day after the funeral.

"But, Elijah, it is. I milked twice yesterday," she'd pointed out.

"I'm not going to anyway."

"Elijah, you have to."

"No, I don't. I don't like milking. Eben Baylor and I made slingshots. We're going hunting."

"Not till you milk. Ma always made you take your turn."

Elijah's face had suddenly twisted. "You're not Ma," he shouted, "and don't you try to boss me." Then he turned and ran from her, stumbling over a fallen log.

Hannah stood there shaking. She felt as though her insides had been pulled out. It was a hateful thing for Elijah to say. As if she thought to set herself up in Ma's place. As though she'd do that! She was only trying to get him to help.

The morning before she died, Ma had said, "Elijah will help if you put it to him right." She'd told Ma he wouldn't, and Ma had said, "Yes, he will."

Well, Ma had been wrong. There would be no help from Elijah.

When Elijah came swaggering back with two squirrels

around noontime looking to be told how smart he was, Hannah gave him no notice. She cooked the squirrels because Andrew and Liddy were hungry, but she didn't eat any of the meat herself.

Since then, she hadn't asked Elijah to do anything. If she didn't, he couldn't sass her, but it was hard doing all the chores that Ma had made him share. Every day Hannah grew more tired and more resentful that Elijah wasn't helping. She'd spoken nice about the milking until he'd started sassing her. What other "right way" was there? And why should Elijah need a right way when it was as plain as the nose on his face that there was more to do than she could do alone?

Well, she'd probably never learn to get work out of Elijah, but there was one thing she did know. She mustn't let on she was having trouble with him or that things were hard. Ma wanted them all to stay together, and she'd warned that folks would try and separate them if it looked as if she couldn't manage. So when anyone asked how they were getting along, Hannah always said, "Just fine. The younger ones help a lot, and we have enough money to do us till Pa gets back."

There was no need to say that she hadn't found the money Ma had talked about and that Elijah only did what suited him.

Milking didn't suit Elijah. Neither did hoeing corn. Weeds had been growing between the rows ever since the fire, and Hannah was on her way to deal with them one morning when Mrs. Baylor stopped her. Liddy had come along in hopes of finding Tabby, and Andrew was taking Magnolia to pasture on the Common.

After a few remarks that didn't mean anything special, Mrs. Baylor got down to what was on her mind.

"You're trying your best, I know, Hannah," she said, "but it's too much to expect of a girl your age to do for a whole family." She fixed her eyes on Liddy and went on. "So long as I can't take Amy until she's weaned, I think your ma would want me to take Liddy. To keep her clean and see she gets to meeting regular." She sniffed. "It isn't nice for a little girl to be so dirty."

For a moment Hannah had no words. She'd hoped she had made it seem she was managing all right. She'd hoped she wouldn't have to think of what to say if what Ma had warned about really happened. But Liddy *was* dirty. She could pretend all she liked about Elijah helping and about the money, but there was no way of denying Liddy was dirty. They all were.

Only the fear that Liddy would answer for herself put words back into Hannah's mouth.

"Thank you kindly, ma'am, but Ma wanted for us all to stay together. It was almost the last thing she said. She wouldn't have wanted us to be dirty, though. I'm planning on doing a big wash this afternoon, and we will all be at meeting on the Sabbath."

Hannah hadn't even thought of washing, but she knew that now she'd have to find time for that, as well as the things she had planned.

At their doorstep in the village Andrew left his sisters to take Magnolia onto the Common, and Hannah and Liddy went past the empty cellar and the blackened heap that had once been the barn. A short way back was a quarter acre of corn. They hadn't managed to plant as much as when Pa was home, and they needed every bit of it.

At first after Ma died, Hannah hadn't thought more than a couple of hours ahead. She did what had to be done to get through each day, but she'd been too weighed down by grief and weariness for more than that. This morning, though, she'd wakened, knowing it wasn't enough. There were things that had to be done for the days ahead as well. They had to have corn, for one thing, and other winter vegetables that were being choked by weeds. Yesterday she'd seen a hoe lying in the grass by the first row of corn when she was looking for eggs. Leaving it there instead of putting it away had been careless of Elijah, but it had saved it from burning.

Next door the Slawsons were working at cleaning up. Mr. Slawson had been out with the militia at the time of the fire, but he was back now. His term of enlistment was up, and he wasn't going to reenlist for a while.

"Good morning, Hannah," he called out when he saw her and she called back, "Good morning, sir."

And suddenly it was a good morning. Not since Ma died had Hannah felt there was anything good in any morning. But this one was. It was as if she'd forgotten there were things to be glad of and had just been reminded. The sun was shining bright, and she took a moment before she went to work to enjoy the feel of it on her back and the look of it on Liddy's honey-colored hair. Dirty or not, Liddy was a darling, and she loved her. She loved Andrew, too, and when she got to know Amy better, maybe she'd love her as much as them. Elijah was ornery, but in time he might improve.

She drew some water for the chickens, and as the bucket came up creaking, she smiled.

"See how many eggs you can find, Liddy," she said, "and afterward look around for a bar of soap. I carried one out from the house, but I haven't seen it since the fire. It may be somewhere in the grass near the well."

"I have to look for Tabby, too," Liddy said.

"Of course you do," Hannah agreed, though it seemed more and more unlikely that the cat was still alive.

When Andrew returned from the Common, Hannah set him to hoeing corn. He wasn't strong enough to keep at it long, but it gave her time to poke around in the debris from the barn. She found the head of another hoe and the metal parts of other things that might be useful if fixed up. Later she'd come back and sort them out, but for now she took the hoe head. It would be good for loosening garden weeds too tough to pull just by hand.

She traded tools with Andrew and started him weeding cabbages. Then she began where he'd left off between the rows of corn. As she chopped at the weeds, old Fred and his hens followed, eyes bright and greedy for any grubs or beetles she might turn up. The corn was nearly shoulder high and, except for the weeds, looked good. If Pa got back in time to harvest it, he'd have plenty to take to the mill for meal, as well as to grind some for Magnolia and the chickens.

When Hannah came to the end of the first row, she straightened before she went on. Liddy was still looking for eggs or maybe for Tabby over by the apple trees. Andrew was squatting among the cabbages, lower lip tucked under upper teeth as he concentrated on his task. Losing either of them was unthinkable, even if Ma hadn't made her promise to keep the family together. But unless Pa got home or she herself could lay things up for winter, they'd have to split up in spite of that. Without food she couldn't stand out against Mrs. Baylor or anyone else.

In the pocket of Hannah's apron was a letter to Pa. She'd written it the day Ma died, sharpening a goose quill and mixing ink from soot. She'd used the paper Amy's christening dress had been wrapped in but she hadn't found anyone yet to take it below British lines. Pa didn't know that Ma was gone. Sometimes Hannah had an urge to tear the letter up. Maybe it would be too much for him to bear when he couldn't do anything but grieve and worry.

With the sun warm but not yet hot and the weeds falling under the chop of her hoe, Hannah thought ahead. They'd need a place that wouldn't freeze to store things for the winter, and Magnolia and the chickens would need protection from wind and snow. So would they.

By the end of the fifth row Hannah began to work things out. They could use the cellar if they cleaned it out and roofed it over. The outside door to the cellar was big enough for Magnolia, and because the ground sloped, there were only a few steps down. If Pa didn't get home in time to rebuild, they all could live there this winter. She still hadn't touched the two dollars in the needle case, and Ma had spoken of more as if maybe it was a lot. Enough for boards and nails?

By the time the sun was overhead Hannah had admitted that she couldn't carry out her plans alone and she'd need Elijah to help her. It wasn't right that he should need things put to him in a special way, but if she wanted him to work, she'd have to think of the way to put it.

"Hannah, I'm hungry." Liddy appeared at the end of the row, half hidden by long green leaves. "I didn't find Tabby, but I found a lot of eggs and the bar of soap."

"All right, lovey. I'm hungry, too," Hannah said. "We'll come back tomorrow and you can look some more for Tabby. You're a smart girl to have found the soap. This afternoon I'll do a big wash, and we'll all be clean enough to suit Mrs. Baylor."

"Hannah?" The small face was worried. "You won't let Mrs. Baylor take me, will you? I don't like her."

"I won't let anyone take you," Hannah promised. "We belong all together like Ma said."

Food and shelter for the winter were a large problem, but it wasn't immediate. An immediate, though much smaller, one was getting them all clean. Ma had done the last wash, and the big kettle hadn't been filled since then. And this morning the fire had been out when they woke because Elijah hadn't brought wood enough to see it through the night and she hadn't made him or done it herself.

Life couldn't go on like this, Hannah decided. For the sake of them all, she had to do something.

As they walked back to Indian Hill, Andrew saw Aaron coming toward them and darted off. Then he came running back. "Hannah, can I have dinner with the Isaacs' and play Indians afterward?" he asked. "Liddy is invited, too, and I'll go for Magnolia before it's time to milk."

"You don't have to," Hannah told him. "I made you a trade this morning. Weeding against evening chores. So run along both of you, and tell Rachel I'll be over later on."

A trade, Hannah mused. Could that be the right way with Elijah? It worked with Andrew. Why not try it?

So when she found him at the shelter making a snare out of sticks and string, she put it to him. "Elijah, if you bring water from the stream and get the fire going again, I'll wash your clothes for you."

Without looking up he replied, "I don't want my clothes washed, and I'm busy."

Hannah tried to keep her voice patient, as though he were Andrew. "Ma would want you clean." She was about to go on and explain about Mrs. Baylor, but Elijah didn't wait.

"Don't tell me what Ma would want," he said belligerently. "You don't know any better than me, and I say she'd want me to finish what I'm doing. It's important. It's—" But Hannah didn't wait either. Her voice rose in exasperation.

"All right then, Elijah. *I* want you clean. I want us all clean. So just you go fetch me that water and fix up the fire."

"No." Elijah's face was set. "I don't have to do what you want. Pa just said to mind Ma."

"Pa?"

"Yes, Pa. When he went off last time, he said to mind Ma but that now I was the man of the family. So I don't have to mind you. I'm the one who should say what to do."

Elijah's words hit Hannah without warning. She believed him about Pa, and that only made things worse. She couldn't think what to do. For a minute she was tempted to forget the wash. But she couldn't. Their spare clothes were as dirty as the ones they were wearing, and Mrs. Baylor would be sure to notice.

Taking a shallow pan, Hannah went over to the Slawsons' shelter for live coals. They'd still be in the village, so she knew she wouldn't have to explain about Elijah letting their own fire go out. When she got back, she put the coals in the fireplace and fed them first with twigs and then sticks. Elijah was still fiddling with his sticks and string, but he lifted his eyes for a quick glance of triumph. Hannah felt her gorge rise, but she pretended not to notice.

After the fire was well caught, she went into the woods for larger wood, taking Pa's ax with her. She knew how to use an ax, but it wasn't rightly a girl's work. She hoped Elijah would follow and offer to help when he heard her chopping, but he didn't. He was still sitting by the shelter, twisting string around sticks, when she brought the wood back.

Without speaking, Hannah carried the heavy kettle to the stream by the road. She filled it to the brim, and it bumped against her every step she took as she returned. She had to set it down several times to rest, and each time her anger against Elijah increased.

The fire was blazing when Hannah lugged the kettle the final steps. Silently she collected clothes and put them into it. Then she broke the bar of soap and put a piece of that in with the clothes. All the time she was conscious of Elijah's eyes on her.

Suddenly and without planning it she walked over to him and snatched the string and sticks out of his hands. She threw them into the fire, where flames consumed them before either she or Elijah quite realized what had happened.

CHAPTER 11

"*Hannah, I can't help worrying about you children." Mrs. Isaacs clasped Hannah to her, taking* care not to crush Amy, who was in her sister's arms.

"We will be all right, ma'am. Really we will. It's the way Ma wanted."

Both Mrs. Isaacs and Hannah had been saying almost these exact same words ever since Mr. Isaacs had found a place at the Avery farm ten miles south for his family to board. But Hannah wasn't as sure as she tried to sound.

While the farm team waited, Mrs. Isaacs delayed for a hug and a special word to each of the other Mills children.

"Andrew, the next time Mr. Isaacs comes out to the farm you ride behind him and visit us. Aaron's going to be lost without you.

"Liddy, maybe we can find a kitten for you and bring it in when we come.

"Elijah, I know what a help you will be to Hannah."

Elijah pulled away a little from Mrs. Isaacs' embrace, but he answered, "Yes, ma'am," politely.

Briefly his eyes sought Hannah's. She looked away. Not once had she complained of him, even to the Isaacs, and she had no intention of doing it now. But she wasn't going to agree with Mrs. Isaacs either. That would be lying.

She went over to the wagon. Jacob, holding his father's horse, was standing beside it, talking to Mr. Avery. Aaron was already on the front seat with Mr. Avery, and Rachel with Ben in her lap on the seat behind them. They all were waiting for Mrs. Isaacs, who was retying some bundles and remembering things she'd forgotten.

Hannah looked up at Rachel, trying to smile. They had said their real good-byes the evening before, but she was afraid the tears would come again if Mrs. Isaacs delayed too long. At last, though, Mr. Isaacs stowed the bundles in the back of the wagon and helped his wife up onto the seat with Rachel. Hannah handed her Amy, suddenly reluctant to part with her youngest sister. Since Mrs. Isaacs had been caring for her, Amy had lost her peaked look. She was pretty now, almost as pretty as Ben, the way Ma had said she would be. Hannah wished Ma could see her.

Mr. Avery slapped the reins on the broad backs of his horses. They were off at a trot. Mr. Isaacs mounted his own horse and rode alongside.

"Good-bye, Andrew!"

"Good-bye, Aaron!" The little boys shouted at each other.

"Good-bye, Rachel, take care of yourself," Hannah called, and Rachel called back, "I will, and *you* take care of Jacob."

Hannah couldn't see the wink, but she knew it was there. She was a little embarrassed at the teasing until Jacob answered it.

"I'll see that she does, Rachel. The same care you take. I'll make her knit me some socks and sew up my torn shirts and do a nice big wash every—" He stopped there because the wagon had gone too far for Rachel to hear any more. But he'd turned the teasing around. Everyone knew Rachel didn't do any of those things.

Until the wagon was out of sight those left behind

stood watching it. Except for Elijah, they all felt a little bereft and reluctant to separate.

Liddy pulled at Hannah's skirts. "Is Amy our baby? Or is she the Isaacs' baby now?"

"She's ours, of course, Liddy, but we can't keep her yet."

While she was explaining, she heard Elijah ask Jacob, "Is your pa just riding as far as the farm, or is he going to buy cattle for the army?"

Hannah stopped talking to Liddy. People weren't supposed to ask when Mr. Isaacs was buying cattle. Especially right out in the open. If it came to the notice of Cowboys or Skinners, they would try to steal them. Either where they were collected or on the road. She was about to tell Elijah to hold his tongue when he went on, "Jacob, if you take me with you when you drive to Peekskill, I can be a real help. I'm smart at not letting people see me. I can go on ahead and let you know if any Cowboys or British are around."

When Jacob replied, his voice was raised. "I'll ask my father, Elijah, but he's not out to buy cattle. He says he won't be buying for the army again soon. It's hard to get farmers to take paper money."

Hannah was surprised that Jacob should be telling Elijah all this and in such a loud voice. Then she saw two mounted figures approaching, Tamar and her brother, Elliott.

When they were close, Jacob, pretending he had just recognized the Halsteads, greeted them courteously.

"Rachel has gone, if you came to say good-bye," he told them.

"I made a ruffled apron for her to take," Tamar said without looking at Hannah.

"I'll keep it safe until I ride out or she comes in for a day," Jacob promised.

Hannah wanted to look at the apron, but she kept

her eyes on the ground. She would have liked to make a present for Rachel, too, but she had no material, much less ruffles.

Tamar waited a minute as if hoping Hannah might speak. Then she said, "Good-bye, Jacob," and rode off.

"Stop around, Elijah, and I'll show you my new gun," Elliott offered as he followed his sister.

Andrew was the first to say anything after the Halsteads left.

"You wouldn't go, would you, Elijah? Why didn't you say so?" His voice rose accusingly.

"Why not?" Elijah replied airily. "Just because their uncle is with De Lancey doesn't mean they are against us. I like Tamar and Elliott."

"Well, I don't," Hannah said furiously, "and you're to stay away—"

"Wait, Hannah," Jacob broke in, putting a hand on her arm. His voice was calm, and even calmer when he spoke to Elijah.

"You are probably right about Tamar not being against us. And nobody knows for sure about her father and mother. But it's different with Elliott. I've heard he's just waiting, like me, to be sixteen so he can join up. Only it's De Lancey's Tories he's going to join, not Patriot militia."

"I don't believe it!" Elijah shouted, his face dark with anger. "You just made that up. Or else Hannah did."

Jacob shrugged. "Well, anyway, my advice is to stay away from Elliott. And to mind what you say in front of any Halstead. My father would have had your breeches down if he'd heard you talking so loud about cattle for the army."

"He'd not dare lick me." Elijah glowered. "He's not my pa. He hasn't the right." Then, as Jacob remained silent, his tone changed. "You wouldn't tell him, would you, Jacob?"

Jacob considered, giving Elijah time to worry a little before he said, "No, I don't think they heard you, and if they did, they didn't learn anything."

Elijah sighed with relief. Mr. Isaacs was a stern man when angered. "I wish I was sixteen and could join the militia, or even fourteen. I've heard one of the Westchester Guides is only fourteen."

"Drummers can be even less," Andrew said, suddenly excited. "I've seen them when infantry and artillery come through. Hannah, can I be a drummer? Please!"

"That would be a fine sight," Elijah mocked. "The drum would be bigger than you."

"It would not!" Andrew's underlip shot out. He looked about to cry.

"Of course it wouldn't," Hannah said. "But if the war keeps going on and on, you both may be old enough to join as regular soldiers before it ends."

"I don't want to wait," Elijah complained. "I want to do something important right now."

You can help me hoe corn and clean up the yard and cellar! The words were hot on Hannah's tongue, but she held them back. Ma wouldn't have wanted her to row with Elijah in front of Jacob. And then she wondered if the help she wanted from Elijah was worth a row. Would the corn actually be harvested? Was the cleaning up of any use?

"Jacob," she asked, "do you think when Bedford is rebuilt, Cowboys and Skinners will come back? Do you think the British will burn it down again?"

"I don't know, Hannah," Jacob answered honestly. "I hope not, but I don't know. But I do know Bedford can't be really safe unless the whole country is safe. What happens across the Hudson or in Connecticut or Massachusetts or New Jersey or in the South can decide whether there will even be a Bedford."

Hannah thought about this later as she was hoeing

corn. It was easier to understand than most of what Jacob had to say about the war. It put things plainly. It gave more reason for Moylan going off to Norwalk in Connecticut. It gave more importance to the American capture of Stony Point across the Hudson that Jacob had tried to tell her about.

Jacob hadn't said it was safe to rebuild, but the Isaacs' had already started. As men from the militia came back, more and more families were getting ready to rebuild. Yards looked cleaner, and the smell of dead animals was gone.

The hoe hit a stone and jarred Hannah's arm. She waited until it stopped tingling. People had to rebuild or abandon their land. Who could afford that? Certainly not Pa. And it would mean leaving Ma behind.

Hannah attacked the weeds again and with more energy. She'd finish the corn herself, but tomorrow she would make Elijah start cleaning out the cellar and the yard. How she'd do it she didn't know. Since she'd burned his snare, they'd hardly spoken a civil word to each other. But she'd find a way, civil or not.

The Baylors had come down to the village and were working next door. Eben was there, and so were the younger boys. Mrs. Baylor had given them all jobs, and she was seeing they did them without any nonsense. She took time herself, though, to come to the edge of the yard and call over to Hannah every now and then.

"Mr. Baylor will be home next week. Any news of your Pa?"

"Where's Elijah? Why isn't he helping hoe?"

"When are you going to start cleaning up? You ought to get that done."

Hannah answered whenever she was close enough so Mrs. Baylor would know she heard, but she stayed in the far end of the field as much as she could instead of hoeing the length of each row.

The Slawsons were different. At noon Mrs. Slawson asked Hannah and Andrew and Liddy to come over and share with her family. She said nice things about how good the corn looked and what a help Liddy and Andrew were getting to be, for five- and six-year-olds. She didn't even mention Elijah, and the only question she asked was one Hannah didn't mind answering.

"Hannah, have you seen any strangers around lately?"

"Why, no, ma'am, I haven't."

"I have," Andrew said unexpectedly, wiping his mouth on his sleeve.

"When, Andrew?" Hannah asked.

He chewed slowly and then swallowed. "This morning early when I brought Magnolia to the Common. A man came up and said he'd pay me a penny a hundred for any nails I found."

"Oh, Andrew. You don't just *find* nails!" Hannah exclaimed. "Nails belong to people even if they're all mixed up with ashes and dirt. You can't sell other people's things. It would be wrong."

"I won't then," Andrew said. "I'll just hunt for pirates' treasure. The man said he'd pay for that, too. He said pirates had buried some here years ago before Bedford was even settled."

Mrs. Slawson and Hannah looked at each other. It was a story to excite a small boy's greed and dull his conscience at the same time. There wasn't any truth in it, but some people did have things hidden in the ground. Usually under a bush where they wouldn't be disturbed. Ever since the Cowboys and Skinners had first started raiding, it had been a fairly common practice.

"Have you lost anything, Mrs. Slawson, ma'am?" Hannah asked.

"No." The woman shook her head. "We had nothing except what was in the house, but this morning the earth was newly turned around the rose bush. Mr. Slawson didn't do it or any of the children."

"Andrew." Hannah leaned toward him. "Would you know the stranger if you saw him again? Think. It's important."

Andrew thought. "I guess so," he said. "Now can I go and play with the others before I have to work some more?"

Mrs. Slawson smiled. "I'm sure Hannah will let you. There is no pirate treasure, Andrew. Only what Bedford people may have buried themselves to keep outlaws from stealing. If you see the stranger again, don't talk to him, but tell your sister right away. Or me."

Andrew scampered off to the end of the yard to join Liddy and the Slawson children. Soon Hannah returned to her hoeing. She was almost finished. But before she was done, she had a thought. She left the corn and went to the lilac bush by the cellar steps. Was this what Ma had tried to tell her before her mind went flighty? Frantically she started digging.

CHAPTER 12

There was nothing under the lilac bush except roots and Hannah knew she'd been foolish to hope there would be. Ma had kept their money in a cracked blue teapot on the top shelf of the pine cupboard. She wouldn't have had time to bury it when she got word the British were coming.

Hannah rose from her knees and brushed the dirt off her skirt. Then she finished the corn and told Andrew he could stop weeding.

"I'd just as soon keep on," he said. "Now Aaron's gone, I can't play Indians with him. It's going to be awful lonesome without the Isaacs'."

"Yes, it is." Hannah felt tears rising and turned away so Andrew wouldn't see them. The evening that lay ahead would be the loneliest since Ma had died. Rachel wouldn't be coming over for milk, and after supper she and Andrew and Liddy wouldn't go over to the Isaacs' shelter to say good-night to Amy. Mrs. Isaacs always kissed them when they left. Tonight she'd miss that kiss so much that likely she wouldn't sleep but just lie awake, thinking of Ma and how maybe she couldn't keep her promise to her.

Walking back to Indian Hill with Liddy's hand in hers and Andrew trudging soberly beside them instead of running ahead to find Aaron, Hannah felt tired and discouraged. While digging, she was so sure she would find the money that she'd had it already spent in her mind on things they would need for winter. Shoes and warm clothes for them all. Hay for Magnolia to replace what had burned in the barn. Boards to cover over the cellar. It was hard to give up the safety this had promised. It would have meant they could stay together for sure the way Ma wanted. Even if Pa didn't get home.

Late in the afternoon, when Andrew and Liddy returned to the village for Magnolia, Hannah started looking around the shelter. She'd looked before but not very hard. The money wouldn't be hidden, she was pretty sure of that. It wasn't Ma's way to hide things from her children. She would have put the money somewhere for safekeeping, like in the needle case, but she wouldn't have really hidden it.

Hannah didn't know exactly how much money there had been, although she could have looked in the teapot at any time before the fire. She expected, however, it might be quite a lot because Pa made good money as a carpenter between times in the militia and Ma made money, too, especially when there was American army around to bake for. Most of it, she supposed, would be in paper notes.

Hannah was leafing through the pages of the Bible when she came on a letter from Pa instead of the paper money for which she was searching. She read the date and then forgot about the money. This was Pa's last letter written from prison four months ago in April. Ma had read it out loud to them, but now Hannah wanted to read it again. Pa had become almost a shadow. She always said, "when Pa gets home," as if she meant it, but as time went on, it seemed less likely, and he seemed less real. Even when she wrote him, she didn't feel his realness. Reading the letter might bring him close again, and right now she had a deep longing for a parent.

Hannah unfolded the sheets of paper. At first the words went as she remembered. Pa said he thought of them all and hoped they were well. He said they should hire the Amblers' yoke of oxen to plow and harrow a piece of ground for planting corn. Then came a sentence Hannah didn't remember.

"A corporal in our room died two days ago. They still haven't taken him out." Hannah stared at the words, shocked by them. Ma hadn't read this part out loud. Oh, no, she hadn't! And between other remembered sentences there was more that Ma had skipped. Hannah read with mounting horror.

"A rat drowned in our pail of drinking water. The jailer wouldn't bring us any fresh."

"A lieutenant from Drake's militia was beaten senseless yesterday because he was thought to be planning escape."

"The sore on my leg is still festering. There are so many of us in one room we can hardly turn around, but we are lucky to have a surgeon's mate here with us. Poor fellow has consumption and may not live long, but meantime he makes a good poultice from bread. It is moldy and full of maggots and no ways fit to eat. But we do eat it."

Suddenly Hannah started shaking. She shook and shook, and she couldn't stop.

Then Jacob was there. He had come for milk. He let his bucket drop, and it clattered on the ground.

"Hannah, what is it?" His voice was sharp with worry. "Is it the fever?"

She didn't answer so he walked over and put a hand on her forehead. It felt cool enough, but she kept on shaking.

"What is it? Please tell me, Hannah." She still didn't answer, but she held out the letter. Jacob took it and read it through.

"Oh, Hannah," was all he said at first as he put an arm around her to stop the shaking.

When she'd calmed a little, he asked, "Didn't you know how things are at the Sugar House? Didn't your mother show you this letter when it came?"

Hannah gulped. "Ma read it to us. But just the good parts. She always said the British treated prisoners well. I thought Pa would be all right till he got exchanged."

Jacob's grip tightened, but neither said anything more until the silence was broken by the slow plop-plop of Magnolia's hooves and Liddy's high-pitched voice. Jacob went to meet the children.

"Hannah's not feeling good," he told them. "I'll do the milking." Liddy's eyes grew frightened, and she ran to throw her arms around her sister.

"Hannah, don't die," she begged. "Please don't."

"I won't, Liddy. I'll be all right pretty soon."

"That's good." Comforted, Liddy's thoughts turned to her stomach. "I'm hungry."

"My mother left a big pot of stew. Father isn't back, and there's too much just for me. I'll go and get it after I've milked," Jacob offered.

Hannah looked at him gratefully. She couldn't seem to control the convulsive shuddering that laid hold of her every time she thought she'd done with it.

Maybe Pa's leg had worsened. Maybe they'd sawed it off. Maybe he'd died, and they'd just let him lie there on the floor for days like the corporal. How could Ma have kept such worry to herself and acted so cheerful in front of them all? Why hadn't she *made* Pa take parole? Why? Why?

Jacob tethered Magnolia to a tree and sat down on a stump to milk. Hannah heard Andrew talking to him and Jacob answering, but her mind wasn't on their words. It was down in New York City with Pa.

Pa couldn't stay in the Sugar House! Was he really so stubborn about parole, or could Ma have tried harder?

Jacob finished milking. He poured half of what he'd milked into his own pail and then looked over at Hannah.

"Feeling any better?" he asked. She nodded, though she really wasn't.

"I'll be right back with the stew," he said. "It will warm you up. Maybe help the shaking. Andrew, put more wood on the fire while I'm gone."

Hannah closed her eyes and then opened them again quickly. Against her lids she'd seen a rat swimming around and around in a pail of water. Ma had never let on how she worried about Pa. But she wasn't strong like Ma. How could she hide her worrying from the younger ones? How could she keep it inside her and never let it out?

Just as Jacob returned with the stew, Elijah brought in two rabbits. Hannah took one look at them hanging limp from his hand and went into the shelter.

"What's the matter with her?" Elijah asked. "Can't she even say thank you when I bring home meat?"

"She will," Jacob said. "Right now she's not feeling good."

While the stew heated over the fire, Jacob helped Elijah skin and clean the rabbits. Andrew and Liddy looked on. Hannah could see them and hear what they said, but none of it seemed real enough to think about. Real was Pa being sick and hungry and thirsty, if he wasn't already dead.

"You must have a good eye to have killed these with a slingshot," Jacob's voice came to her.

"I have," Elijah boasted. "If I had a gun like Elliott's, I could knock down Britishers as easy as rabbits." Then his voice lowered. "Jacob, if Elliott will lend me his gun, can I come along when your father takes the cattle he's buying to the army?"

This conversation came to Hannah as from a distance. An unimportant background against which she was desperately searching for a way for Pa to escape death.

Escape. *Escape from prison!* Was that the way if Pa still held out against parole? Then Hannah saw a bloody figure shoved back into a crowded room. Drake's lieutenant? Or was it Pa?

"I'm not talking loud. No one can hear." Elijah's voice intruded.

"I said my father wasn't buying," Jacob replied.

"But that was in case someone heard. I know he's buying."

"You do, Elijah?" Andrew's voice was excited. "How?"

"I won't tell. Not anyone. Not if I was tortured even." Elijah sounded as though he were trying to impress Jacob rather than annoy Andrew.

Jacob said something, and then Andrew interrupted. "Well, then, I won't tell you about the stranger. The one that wants to buy nails and things for hard money."

"What?" Now it was Elijah's turn to sound excited. "How much will he pay?"

"A lot. He wants other things, too. Things that are buried under bushes," Andrew said.

"Well, don't fall for his game, either of you," Jacob warned. "He's looking for boys to do his stealing for him. That's what. I've heard of his kind. They come like buzzards after a burning. They sell to British or Tories or Whigs, and they don't care which." Then his tone changed. "What does the stranger look like, Andrew?"

Andrew sounded confused. "I'm not real sure anymore. But I can remember what he said. He told me to leave three stones in the hole of that tree by the Slawsons' if I found anything to sell him."

A while later Jacob came into the shelter bringing a bowl of stew. "Better eat this, Hannah," he said. "You'll need it. Elijah says you and he are going to start clearing up around your cellar tomorrow."

"Elijah said that!" Hannah exclaimed.

"Why, yes." Jacob sounded surprised. "Hadn't you figured on starting so soon?"

Hannah looked past Jacob's big solid body at Elijah. What had got into him? Was he just tired of his own orneryness, or did clearing up seem important, now Jacob, four years his elder, had started at the Isaacs'?

Well, whichever, she was glad of it. Neither reasoning nor losing her temper had any effect on Elijah. She'd found no way to make him work, and now she didn't have to. He'd offered.

"Yes, we are figuring on it. Elijah and I are starting tomorrow," she said as if she'd been sure of it all the time.

Tomorrow she wouldn't have to make excuses for Elijah so Mrs. Baylor didn't guess he was no help. He'd be right there working with her where everyone could see. Soon she was bound to find the money Ma had put away, and with Elijah helping, she could manage. Not just pretend so neighbors wouldn't try and take the children. If Pa did live and did get home, he'd find them all together.

"I'll be going now." Jacob hesitated. "Hannah, I'm sorry for what the letter said, but I'm glad you showed it to me."

Hannah came back to the present, aware of Jacob's eyes on her.

"Maybe I shouldn't have." Then words she didn't mean to say came rushing out. "Oh, Jacob, I can't let on to the younger ones, but I'll have to talk about Pa to someone."

"You can talk to me," Jacob said. "I want you to, Hannah. Any time you have a need to talk about him."

When he left the shelter, Hannah got to her feet, intending to have a word with Elijah before they slept. But Elijah was following Jacob toward the road. She was asleep when he returned.

CHAPTER 13

With Elijah working beside her, it was easy for Hannah to overlook the things he wouldn't do. If he didn't choose to milk or do chores around the shelter, at least that gave him longer hours to work in the village.

The morning after she read Pa's letter, Hannah woke to find Elijah gone. So much of the evening before seemed hazy that she wondered if Elijah had really told Jacob he intended to start at clearing up and if Jacob had really repeated that to her. But when she and Andrew and Liddy reached the village, Elijah was already there. He was pulling charred pieces of timber out of the cellar and piling them on the grass. Sweat trickled down his begrimed face, and his shirt stuck to his body.

Hannah and Elijah had become unused to talking pleasantly, and it was difficult to start again. Hannah made the first move at reconciliation. "I'm glad of your help, Elijah," she said. "I couldn't lift that heavy wood alone like you do. You're stronger than I am."

After that, talking was easier. Hannah explained how roofing over the cellar would give them a place to live until they could rebuild. And that they had to find the money Ma had saved so they could buy the things they needed for winter. She was listing the things they'd need when a strident voice interrupted.

"Well, I see you have Elijah working at last," Mrs. Baylor shouted from the lot next door.

Elijah scowled, and Hannah answered quickly. "It was Elijah's idea to start on the cellar today, ma'am."

Mrs. Baylor's eyes went past Elijah to Andrew and Liddy, who were at the lower end of the yard. Andrew had drawn water from the well and was filling a dish for the chickens. Liddy was carrying some of it in her cupped hands for a broody hen who wouldn't leave her nest in the long grass.

They were too far away for Mrs. Baylor to examine them closely, but she couldn't go back to her own business without a parting shot.

"Mind you now, Hannah, I expect to see all of you at meeting tomorrow. And clean."

"Yes'm." Hannah gave Elijah a warning look and bit her own lips to keep from a tart reply. They would be at meeting tomorrow all right, and they would be clean. Their Sabbath clothes were already washed and folded neat between two quilts in the shelter. For more than once Hannah felt grateful that the Hessian officer had given them time to save so much. Lots of people didn't have a change of clothes.

Hannah was proud of the way her family looked the next morning when the congregation gathered in the burying ground for worship. Even Elijah hadn't fussed about making himself clean. He and Andrew had gone to the river to bathe, and Hannah and Liddy had washed with hot water at the shelter. At first, after Ma died, it had been hard to go to meeting, remembering the sadness of the funeral. But now, a month later, it brought comfort and strength. It was nice having it outdoors under the sky, she thought, with nothing between them and heaven. When the pastor went on too long in his drony voice, Hannah let her mind wander and looked up at the fluffy white clouds. That's where Ma was and the twins and the other babies who'd died too young to get acquainted with. They'd be happy to have Ma with them again, and Hannah at last could think about it without pain. She wouldn't ever forget Ma, but she was ready to let go of her.

Then the pastor began praying. Not the prayers about paths of righteousness and dens of iniquity, but the ones for special people. He prayed for General Washington and for all the soldiers in the American army. He prayed for those in battle. And then he prayed for those in prison. He always did, but the words had never struck at Hannah's heart as they did now. Before, "strength and patience to endure hardship" had meant the long waiting for exchange and Pa's longing to be with his family. But not now. Now it meant rats and hunger and a festering sore that wouldn't heal.

Staring ahead at Ma's grave but not really seeing it, Hannah clenched her hands so tight her nails bit into her palms. When meeting was over, she told Liddy and Andrew to walk home with the Slawsons and went to find Jacob. He was in the Isaacs' yard, fitting a makeshift handle onto the blade of a shovel.

"Pa can't stay in the Sugar House," she said when she stood beside him. "He can't just keep on waiting for exchange. He'll . . ." Her voice had been firm and determined, but now it faltered. "Oh, Jacob, I'm so scared he'll die first!"

Jacob's eyes held sympathy and understanding, but he didn't try for a soft reply.

"It could be he will," he said honestly, "but we have to hope he won't."

"No! Hoping's not enough. Neither is praying." Hannah was shocked by her own words, but she went right on. "I'll ask God for help, but it's me that has to do it."

"Do what, Hannah?"

"Make Pa change his mind about parole. It was offered in the beginning. He has only to ask."

Jacob looked at her a while before he spoke. "He was in Colonel Thomas' regiment when they both were taken prisoner."

"Yes." Everyone knew that. What was Jacob getting at?

"Colonel Thomas broke his parole to fight again."

"Yes." Everyone knew that, too. Then Jacob's meaning came to her. She looked at him questioningly and he said, "After that happened, they might figure your father would do the same."

"Not Pa!" Hannah exclaimed. "Pa would never break his word."

"Likely they'd not believe that. Besides, your mother said over and over he wouldn't ask because he wouldn't promise not to fight against the British again."

"But that was before Bedford burned. Before Ma died. When he hears about Ma, he will think different maybe. Even if they paroled him in the city or on Long Island, they'd give him leave to come home a few days. Lieutenant Smith said so. He'd want that—to see how we are doing—don't you think so, Jacob?"

"Hannah, doesn't he *know* about your mother?"

She shook her head. "I wrote about Bedford. Major Tallmadge took that letter. Later I wrote about Ma." She pulled the letter out of her pocket. "I carry it with me always, but I haven't found anyone to take it yet."

"Give it to me then," Jacob said. "I can help with that anyway. Father and I are riding over to the Hudson soon. After we deliver the cattle, I'll find an officer who will send it for you. Sheldon and Tallmadge are south of Peekskill somewhere on the lines, I've heard. I'll ride as far as I have to."

"Oh, Jacob, thank you!" Hannah held out the letter and then drew it back. "I'll give it to you tomorrow. I need to write a new one. When I wrote this, I didn't know how bad things were with Pa and that he might die if he didn't get out soon. I just said things Ma would have wanted. How kind everyone was and how he shouldn't worry. I've got to change that."

She stopped and took a deep breath. "I'm going to tell Pa we can't do without him. That we've got to have one parent we can count on living. I'm going to tell him he's got to think of us. I can't just do what Ma would want anymore. I've got to decide what's right myself."

Jacob studied her as though she were someone different. "Yes, you have to do that," he said. Then he smiled. "And I'd say you are plenty able to, Hannah."

It was good to have a friend like Jacob, Hannah thought as she walked back toward the shelter and suddenly felt surprise that she was thinking of Jacob as her friend. He'd always been friendly, but Rachel had been her friend, and he'd just been Rachel's older brother. Now he was her friend, too. She didn't know how it had happened, but it made her feel less alone.

When she reached Indian Hill, Hannah found Elijah inside the shelter. He was feeling in the crevices at the back of the rock wall. When he saw her, he said, "I'm looking for the money you said Ma put somewhere."

"I'll look, too." Maybe both of them looking together would turn up what she hadn't found alone. But except for the money in the needle case, which Elijah hadn't known about before, they didn't find any.

After a while Elijah changed into everyday shirt and pants and went off to meet Eben Baylor. Eben was a showoff and a bragger, and Hannah didn't like him, but so long as Elijah was working hard and keeping away from the Halsteads, she wasn't going to say anything against what he did in his spare time.

Elijah went on working hard. He got up every morning at first daylight and put in several hours of work in the village while most people were still at the shelters. Sometimes he stayed until dark. Everything was going so well that Hannah almost forgot there had ever been hard feelings between them.

One close overcast day they carried the last of the charred wood and bricks and rubble out of the cellar. It was dirty work, and before noon Hannah felt tired and hot and itchy. She went to the well for water to drink and splash on her face and arms. As she was pulling up the bucket she heard horses coming along the road and turned to see who it was. The next moment she looked away, but not before she'd seen that the riders were Tamar and Elliott Halstead. Tamar was staring straight ahead between the ears of her little brown mare. Elliott smiled and raised a hand in greeting. Turning her back on them, Hannah faced the cellar. Standing beside it, Elijah had a hand raised in reply. The look in his eyes was too friendly for her liking, but before he spoke or took a step toward the road, Tamar put her horse into a gallop. Elliott followed.

A week ago Hannah would have accused Elijah of staying friends with the Halsteads against her orders, but now she held her tongue. She couldn't afford a new falling out with Elijah with so many other things to worry about. Pa, and not finding the money, and lately the thieving that was going on. All over the village things were missing. Metal parts of tools, nails and hinges disappeared almost as soon as they were dug up from foundations of houses and barns. People took to burying them like valuables to keep them safe, but they disappeared anyway. Hannah and Elijah carried every piece of metal they could use again back to the shelter because they couldn't risk losing as much as a single nail. Elijah was earning a few pennies helping other families, but it would never be enough for what they needed.

Strangers passing through the burned-out village got hard looks, but no one ever saw any of them take anything, except once when a couple of ragged infantry soldiers stole a hen and ran off with it.

When Jacob came by for milk one evening, he questioned Andrew about the stranger who had offered to pay for nails and buried treasure.

"Have you ever seen the man again?" he asked.

Andrew shook his head. "No. I'd have told Hannah or Mrs. Slawson right away. I promised."

Hannah stripped the last drops of milk from Magnolia. "Maybe he didn't come back because Andrew didn't put stones in the hole of the Slawsons' tree," she suggested.

"There are stones there. Three stones." Liddy glanced up from the tiny house she was building out of twigs. "I found them this afternoon when I was looking for a place to keep treasures."

"What treasures?" Hannah's voice was sharp in sudden alarm. Had Liddy been thieving like a little magpie? Did that account for some of the things that were missing in the village?

"These." Liddy fished in her apron pocket and brought out a broken piece of ruby glass and two small pieces of china. "Did I do wrong to take them, Hannah?" Liddy's lower lip was trembling.

Hannah gathered her little sister in her arms, hugging her tight in relief. "It's all right, Liddy. Only don't take things from other people's cellars, and show me what you find."

"Did you leave the stones in the tree?" Jacob asked.

Liddy nodded. "Yes. I decided not to use the hole for my treasures. I'm building a house for them instead."

Jacob poured some of the milk from Hannah's pail into his own and then set it down. "I'm going back to the village," he said. "I'll be by for this later. If the stones are still in the tree, I'll keep watch till the stranger shows up and find out who's stealing for him."

"I just hope he comes!" Andrew exclaimed. "Can I help you watch?"

"Better not. I may have to stay hidden all night."

"I wouldn't mind," Andrew assured Jacob.

But Hannah was against it. "Elijah is still down in the village," she said. "He can help watch."

"I won't go to sleep anyway," Andrew protested. "Not till Jacob comes back and tells us what's happened."

Hannah fixed supper from leftover johnnycake and milk. Her supply of cornmeal was getting low, but Mr. Isaacs had promised to bring some more tomorrow. He rode out into the country almost every day. He was spending tonight at the Avery farm. When he came back, he would have news of Rachel and Amy. Soon he and Jacob would start for the Hudson, taking her letter to Pa with them. She had already given it to Jacob. It said what she wanted now.

Andrew and Liddy stayed awake well past their usual bedtimes. It was long after dark when Liddy dropped off and Hannah carried her into the shelter. Andrew held out longer, but finally he rolled himself up in his blanket near the banked fire.

"Wake me when Jacob and Elijah get back," he said, and Hannah promised she would.

Waiting, she sat with her back against a tree. Had the stranger come yet? she wondered. Had he put his hand into the hole and found the three stones? Would he lead Jacob and Elijah to a boy who had stolen things to sell? Who would that be? Certainly not a boy of Andrew's age, who would be missed at bedtime.

Hannah's eyes closed, then opened again. Then closed for a longer time. She wasn't conscious of falling asleep, but she must have or she wouldn't have been so fuzzy-minded when she heard someone blundering through the trees.

Jacob? But it wasn't Jacob. It was Elijah, and he was blubbering as he threw himself on his blanket and wound it around him like a cocoon.

"Elijah! What's the matter?" Hannah roused and went over to him. "Did the stranger hurt you? What happened?"

He didn't answer, and Hannah knelt beside him. "Tell me, Elijah, please."

"Leave me alone," he bawled, clutching the blanket tight over his head.

"Elijah, I have to know. If you're hurt, you have to tell me. Does Jacob know you are hurt?"

Suddenly Elijah unwound himself and jumped to his feet. "That Jacob!" he cried. "I hate him! He had no right!" Still shouting "I hate him," he ran off into the dark. Hannah stood quite still, until she couldn't hear him anymore. Then her legs gave way, and she sat down, hands clasping her knees and her head lowered on them.

"Oh, Elijah," she whispered. "Oh, Elijah."

CHAPTER 14

There had been no suspicion beforehand to lessen Hannah's shock. Elijah's the one Jacob found. Elijah's the thief. Without warning the dreadful words had wrapped themselves around her heart as she watched her brother running off into the night. Now, with head on knees, she felt too stunned to change her position long after it became uncomfortable. The ache in the back of her neck was less than the ache of her shame for Elijah.

It was only when both became unbearable that her mind began a frantic search for reasons why she might be wrong. Perhaps there was some other explanation for Elijah's words and behavior. Jacob could have sent him home, saying he was too young to help. Hannah raised her head. A spark flew up into the sky, and her hopes rose with it. Being treated young would have hurt Elijah's pride and made him angry.

The spark and the hope died at the same time. It wasn't reason enough for such hatred against an older boy he'd always admired. There could be some other reason, though, one that didn't make Elijah a thief. Slowly Hannah got to her feet. If there was another explanation, she needed to know it. If there wasn't, she had to know that, too, and Jacob was the only one who could tell her.

Andrew didn't wake easily. He had slept through Elijah's return and tempestuous departure, and Hannah had to shake him hard to rouse him.

"Did they catch the thief?" he asked in a half-asleep, half-awake voice.

"I don't know," Hannah answered, hoping she didn't. "Andrew, I have to be gone for a while. Will you move inside with Liddy so if she wakes and misses me she won't be scared?"

"Yes'm, Hannah." Rubbing his eyes, Andrew stumbled into the shelter, dragging his blanket behind him.

Hannah poured water over the fire. She'd have to build it new in the morning, but she couldn't risk leaving it alive with Andrew and Liddy alone and asleep. Then, taking Jacob's half-filled milk pail with her, she walked out to the road and up toward the Isaacs' shelter. A sliver of moon gave light enough to see the way except where trees arched overhead. There was no one else on the road and no sound of human voices. A dog barked, and Hannah stood still until it came over. When it sniffed her hand and was satisfied, she went on.

Jacob was standing with his back to her, fixing his fire for the night. Once he stopped as she approached, as though he heard her, but he didn't turn around.

"You forgot to come for your milk. I brought it." Hannah waited for him to turn, hoping his face would tell her that nothing was wrong.

"You didn't have to, Hannah. I'd have come for it in the morning." He bent over to rearrange a stick. "It's not right for you to be here so late. I'll take you home."

Hannah still couldn't see his face, but it didn't matter. If Jacob had caught anyone, it wasn't Elijah. Surely if it were, he'd know why she'd had to come. He wouldn't be disapproving of the hour.

"Did you see the stranger? And the boy stealing for

him?" Released from fear that an answer would implicate Elijah, Hannah could ask the questions she'd avoided.

"The stranger made off when he knew I was following. I didn't recognize him. Let's be going, Hannah." Jacob had turned toward her now, his face and voice both impatient.

"But the boy, Jacob? Did you see him?"

"Yes, I saw him." Jacob didn't offer anything further as she stood there waiting.

"Well, who was he? Tell me, Jacob," Hannah prodded insistently.

"I'm not saying who he was. Not to anyone." Jacob spoke as though the subject were closed, but Hannah wouldn't let be.

"But you'll have to tell someone, Jacob. Else how will he be punished and made to give things back?"

"I don't have to tell, and I'm not going to," Jacob said stubbornly. "All the things are returned—two sacks full. And the boy *is* punished. I did it myself. He'll hurt where he sits for a while, but he won't steal again."

All at once Hannah was back in the nightmare from which she'd escaped.

"Jacob, oh, Jacob! You didn't have his breeches down?"

"I did," Jacob replied. "Who else was there to do it unless I gave his name out?"

"He'll never forgive you. Never," Hannah whispered.

"You are wrong, Hannah. The whole thing is settled and can be forgotten."

"It was Elijah. You can stop trying to hide it, Jacob. I'm sure now because of something he said when he came back from the village. He said you had no right. It was the licking he meant." Hannah's throat was so tight it hurt, but she spoke unflinchingly.

"I'm sorry, Hannah." Jacob looked unhappy. "I didn't

want you to know. It won't do any good that you know. It could do harm."

"Pa will die of shame," Hannah went on as though she hadn't heard him.

"He won't know unless you tell him," Jacob pointed out. "I said I wasn't telling anyone, and Elijah's not likely to."

"Whatever shall I say to Elijah?" Hannah was asking the question of herself, but Jacob answered.

"Nothing. Don't let him guess you know. He has to think you don't know or he can't hold up his head."

"What matter?" Hannah asked wearily. A boy who stole from burned-out neighbors had no right to hold up his head.

"Because he might run away. Even my mother wouldn't think you able to keep the others then. You'd all be split up. This thing is between me and Elijah, Hannah. Let it be."

"I'll think about it, Jacob. It doesn't seem right, but I'll think about it hard. And thank you for saying you won't tell. It would shame Andrew and Liddy, as well as Pa."

"I will take you back now, Hannah."

"No, I'd rather go alone in case Elijah saw."

There wasn't anything more to say, but they stood looking at each other for a moment longer. Jacob took a step forward. Then he turned and went back to the fire.

Hannah walked home slowly. It went against the grain to leave Elijah his pride, but Jacob could be right.

A horse came pounding down the road, and Hannah drew to the side and stood behind a tree. Night riders needn't be friends. Then, as the horse passed by, she realized her fears were groundless. The rider was Mr. Isaacs. He wasn't expected till morning, but it was Mr. Isaacs all right. The light wasn't enough to recognize the face under the hat brim, but she knew him by the lopsided way he sat a horse. He left the road and turned into a field opposite his shelter. At its edge was the shed where he'd kept his two horses after the village burned.

When Hannah reached home, Elijah's blanket lay flat on the ground, not humped as though it covered a boy. She touched it to make sure and then crawled under the coverlet with Liddy.

In the morning Elijah's blanket was rolled up, so she knew he'd been back. But he was gone again. She saw there had been a visitor before she woke. On the rock near the fireplace was a sack of cornmeal and a cake basket. Weighted down by a stone was a letter sealed with wax.

From Rachel! Hannah knew it by the writing. Elijah and the problem of what to do about him would have to be faced, but right now what she wanted most was to put it off and think of something else. Eagerly she broke the seal and unfolded the paper.

"Andrew! Liddy!" She called. "Wake up. Mr. Isaacs brought a letter from Rachel. It tells about Amy!"

When the two younger children joined her, she spread the letter out and read it to them.

Rachel wrote that Amy was getting fat and never spit up any more and hardly ever cried. Mrs. Isaacs had made new dresses, both alike, for Amy and Ben, and some people thought they were twins. The Averys had a fine big house with lots of rooms, and there were other boarders. Mrs. Avery let people use her oven, and Rachel had made the cake she'd sent from a receipt one of the boarders had given her. She hoped Hannah would like it. There was a litter of kittens in the hayloft, and Mr. Avery said Liddy could have one when they were old enough.

"Can we have Amy, too," Liddy asked, "or do we have to choose?"

"We can have both." Hannah ran a hand through

Liddy's tangled curls. "Only with Amy we will have to wait a little longer."

At the end of the letter was a part that Hannah didn't read out loud. "There are two Avery boys, and they are both real handsome. If I didn't plan for you to marry Jacob, I would talk you up to the younger one. I want the older one for myself."

Hannah folded the letter and put it in her pocket. Later she burned it. She couldn't risk anyone reading that silly business about Jacob. Rachel would have to stop it. There was friendship between Jacob and herself now that she didn't want spoiled by teasing.

When Magnolia was milked, Hannah sent Andrew and Liddy to take her to the Common. Without a fire there had been nothing for breakfast but milk and berries, but Andrew had borrowed some coals, and as soon as she got a proper fire again, she planned to boil eggs and bring them with her to the village.

She was on her knees encouraging some dry twigs by blowing on them when she heard someone come up behind her.

"Hannah, I have something to say." It was Tamar's voice.

"Well, I don't want to hear it."

"You had better listen. It's about Elijah."

Hannah got to her feet and turned to face Tamar. So she'd heard about the thieving. If Tamar knew, it was no secret. Others must know, too. Hannah took a deep breath. "Everything's back," she said coldly. "Now please go."

Tamar didn't move. "I don't know what you mean." Her voice was no more cordial than Hannah's. "I came because of Jacob. Rachel's my friend."

"I told you to go." If Tamar hadn't come about the thieving, Hannah didn't care what she had to say about Elijah and Jacob. She didn't have to listen to Tamar talk about Jacob.

Suddenly Tamar had her by the shoulders. For a girl so fragile-looking she had a strength that always took Hannah by surprise.

"No, I won't go. And you have to listen. Unless you want De Lancey to steal the cattle the Isaacs' are driving to the Hudson today."

Anger got in the way of clear thinking. Hannah stared at Tamar, unable to make sense of what she was saying. Tamar went on. "Elijah came to our house very late last night. He pounded on the door and waked us all. He had listened behind a rock to Mr. Isaacs and Jacob talking after Mr. Isaacs got back. He told us the cattle are collected in that hollow behind the Raymonds' barn. He told us how many head there are and the route they are taking to Peekskill."

Tamar paused for breath and then continued. "I came as soon as I could slip out, but there isn't much time. Elliott rode off right after Elijah left to give Uncle Roger the news for Colonel De Lancey. The Isaacs' left as soon as it was light this morning. I saw them pass our house."

"Tamar, it's not true! Why are you saying such a dreadful thing?"

"It is true, Hannah. And I'm telling you because the Isaacs' have been kind. There is another reason, though. One you wouldn't believe." She paused, looking at Hannah straight. "I want those cattle to get to the American army."

There was antagonism in the eyes of both girls as they stood facing each other. Then slowly the expression in Hannah's eyes changed.

Tamar was telling the truth. A terrible truth but more believable than that Elijah should steal. She had told Jacob that Elijah wouldn't forgive him. She'd known he'd try to get even somehow.

"I do believe you, Tamar. Everything you said. The Isaacs' must be warned."

"Yes," Tamar said, her expression also changing. "Only I can't help anymore. Except to lend you my horse. I don't dare. Our family is divided. My father had no part in the burning, but he is still loyal to the king. He wants that drove of cattle to reach the British, not the American army. My mother and I are against the king, but we don't dare cross Father."

Hannah put out a hand and touched her arm. "I wish I'd known, Tamar. I wouldn't have been so mean." It was something she had to say, though Tamar was impatient to finish.

"I have to go now. I'll be waiting on the top of Indian Hill as soon as I saddle my horse. Later I'll tell Father she threw me and ran off."

"Tamar, I saw you ride the other day. You were riding a lady's saddle. I don't know how."

"I have no other now. You will have to ride without."

"It's the way Pa taught us," Hannah replied.

"I'll tell you how to go when we meet on Indian Hill. I can't stay here any longer. I mustn't be seen with you."

Tamar climbed up the cliff, dislodging some pebbles. Hannah ran down the road to the village. Before she left Bedford, she had to arrange for Liddy and Andrew. If Mrs. Slawson couldn't keep them all day, she'd have to ask Mrs. Baylor. But before she asked either, she needed to make up a story. A believable story that had nothing to do with Elijah. Or with Tamar.

CHAPTER 15

Hannah slowed her steps before she reached the first house lot in the village. In spite of the need for hurry, she musn't go faster than a girl would walk who felt headachy and sick. Because that was the reason she'd decided to give in asking Mrs. Slawson or Mrs. Baylor to keep Andrew and Liddy for the day.

The rasp of a saw in the Browns' lot told her they had commenced work on the framework of their new house. Yesterday she would have stopped to watch a minute, but now she went right on by. In the next lot several men were gathered, talking, not working. A snatch of conversation reached her ears.

"Not where I left those latches and nails, but they are back—all of them."

"Mine, too. It don't make sense."

Hannah's cheeks burned hot, and she kept her eyes on the road. She was afraid someone might read her mind and know who had returned the stolen articles. Maybe they'd read in her mind about Elijah turning traitor, too. Traitor was a hard word, but what other was there for a person who gave information to Tories? Even if it was a boy of eleven who did it just to get even for a licking?

"Hannah, have you heard?" Mrs. Baylor shouted as she passed the Baylors' yard. Hannah pretended not to hear and went on. In their own lot she saw Elijah out back by the barn. Andrew and Liddy were near the cellar sifting ashes through their fingers. Neither of them looked up, and she didn't call to them.

Next door Mrs. Slawson was picking pole beans. Her fingers kept busy while she listened to Hannah, but her kind broad face was sympathetic.

"Of course I will keep the young ones for you," she promised. "You just go on back and get a good rest. You have been working too hard, Hannah, and you look downright sick. Maybe being head of a family is too much for a girl your age like Mrs. Baylor says."

"Oh, no, ma'am," Hannah protested quickly. "It's just today—"

"Oh." Mrs. Slawson looked at her understandingly. "Well, best lie down and be quiet. I'll take your young ones back to our shelter when I go, so they won't bother you."

She beckoned to her little boy. "Joshua, go tell Andrew and Liddy they are to come over here and play with you," she directed him.

"Thank you, ma'am, thank you." Hannah felt guilty about lying, but right now she'd had to.

Once out of Mrs. Slawson's sight, her steps quickened. Soon she was running.

Tamar was waiting in the field on top of Indian Hill. She was holding her little brown mare by the length of the reins so she could nibble on grass.

"You have ridden Queenie before, so you know her ways," she said.

"Yes," Hannah replied, putting a hand out to stroke the horse's shoulder. When they'd still been friends, Tamar had let her ride Queenie once in a while. She had never been used for farmwork as were most Bedford horses. Raised for pleasure riding, she was easy-gaited and well mannered. Hannah knew how much Tamar loved the little animal.

"I'll try and be careful of her," she promised, and then suddenly hopeful, she added, "And maybe I won't have far to ride. Maybe the Isaacs' aren't actually moving the cattle till dark for safety and I'll find them still at the Raymonds' just getting things ready."

Tamar shook her head. "Cowboys robbed a farm west of Guard Hill night before last. Elijah heard Mr. Isaacs say he was more worried about meeting up with outlaws on the road at night than he was of traveling in the daytime."

She led Queenie over to a rock so Hannah could get on more easily. When Hannah was mounted, with skirts tucked properly, Tamar gave her the reins but still kept a hand on one, up near the bit.

"If the Isaacs' haven't already started, they will soon," she said. "Ride Queenie as hard as you need, to warn them. Those cattle mustn't be taken. And besides, who knows what De Lancey's men might do to the Isaacs' if they put up a fight?"

Hannah's stomach jumped. Jacob would fight. She knew that. Mr. Isaacs, too. They wouldn't give up the cattle without a struggle.

Tamar went on giving directions. "Mr. Isaacs is driving up over Guard Hill. At the bottom, go right until you come to the house of the old Quaker woman. Do you know where that is?"

Hannah nodded. "Yes, but I've never been any farther."

"Listen, then. You turn left there and go downhill. You won't pass any more houses. It's mostly woods. In about a mile you will ford a brook. Pine's Bridge crosses the Croton River a mile beyond that."

Queenie was getting restless, but Tamar still held onto her.

"Another road comes up from North Castle Church to Pine's Bridge. That's the one De Lancey's party will take. If they don't see cattle tracks at the bridge, they will ride up the road toward the Quaker woman's and wait for the Isaacs' behind a turn."

"Tamar, how do you know?"

"I heard the instructions Father gave Elliott for Uncle Roger. I know this, too. The Refugees are below Tarrytown, but they will ride as fast as they can to catch the Isaacs' on this side of the Croton. They won't want to cross the bridge unless they have to because there's a house on the other side sometimes used as an American outpost."

"Tamar, I'm scared," Hannah said. "I haven't ridden in over a year, except on Lieutenant Smith's Dandy once or twice in back of the barn. What if I can't make Queenie go fast enough? What if I fall off and can't catch her again?"

"I wish I dared go myself, Hannah, but if I'm not home for dinner at noon, Father will want to know why. He mustn't ever guess I had anything to do with warning the Isaacs'. He'd lock me up in my room for days, and he'd never believe Mother wasn't in on the plan."

Briefly Tamar turned away, thinking about her parents. Then, with a little shake of her shoulders, she turned back to Hannah.

"You will be all right, Hannah. You can depend on Queenie. Now you had better go. Here, tie my kerchief over your hair. There is no one at the north end of the village right now to see you on Queenie, but if you should meet anyone, duck your head so all they will see is the kerchief. When you get back, leave Queenie's bridle on the ground where the meetinghouse shed stood. Turn her loose there, and she'll come home. She's my friend." Tamar gave a bitter little laugh. "About my only one, I guess."

She took her hand off Queenie's rein, but Hannah held the horse in a moment longer.

"I want to be your friend again, if you will let me, Tamar," she said a little awkwardly. "Please do."

Tamar nodded, but she didn't speak, and Hannah turned the mare north down the long sloping field to the Salem road. Once there she touched Queenie's side with her heel and gave her her head. They went fast through the crossroads and didn't meet anyone who would recognize either the horse or herself. In spite of her recent misgivings, Hannah found herself as comfortable on Queenie as though she'd been riding her every day. The little mare was easy to sit and willing to do what she asked.

It hadn't rained in two weeks. Dust coated the weeds growing along the sides of the road, but the dust raised by Queenie's hooves was always behind them. The sun was behind them, too, as they rode west. Later it might be hot, but now it was only pleasantly warm on Hannah's back and shoulders.

Until she reached the Raymonds' farm, Hannah let herself hope the Isaacs' had made a late start and she could stop them there from going on. But when she came to an opening in the wall, she saw the cattle had already passed through it. The dusty road was pockmarked with cloven hoofprints and dotted with saucers of dung.

Hannah put Queenie into a gallop, hoping as she topped each rise and rounded each turn, to see cattle ahead of her. But she didn't, and when she came to the very top of the road, she pulled up and let Queenie blow, while her eyes searched the country ahead for a moving cloud of dust. Suddenly she felt Queenie's muscles tighten. She didn't shy, but her ears went forward, and her head swung to the left. A moment later some bushes parted and a man of about sixty came out onto

the road. From the direction he'd come Hannah guessed he was one of the men over militia age who stationed themselves by turn as sentinels on the high elevation south of the road.

From there you could see for miles. Once Hannah had ridden up there with Pa. He had shown her Tarrytown on the Hudson River, thirteen miles away, and much nearer, near enough to make out some of the buildings, even, the little hamlet called North Castle Church. That was the way Tarleton had come when he raided Pound Ridge and the way the enemy came nine days later when they burned Bedford. It was the way De Lancey's Refugees would come to get to Pine's Bridge.

The man stopped beside Hannah and smiled. "Josiah Mills' girl, ain't you? Nice little mare you have there. Want to sell her?"

"No," Hannah replied and added a "thank you" before she asked, "Did you see some cattle pass while you were up there?"

"Sure did. Fifty or sixty head going west. Soon after sunrise and traveling slow as though they had a long way to go."

Sunrise! And it must be close to eight-thirty now. Even going slow like the man said, that meant the cattle were miles ahead of her. If Elliott had found his uncle right away where he expected and if the Refugees had ridden up fast, there mightn't be time to catch up with the Isaacs' before it was too late.

"Did you see anything down by North Castle Church that looked like a troop of horses?" Hannah's heart was in her throat as she asked the question.

"Not me. If I'd seen as much as a handful of dust or a pinpoint of sun on metal, I'd be running to give an alarm right now, not walking home for breakfast."

So there was still time, but maybe not much. Hannah

dug her heels in Queenie's sides and slapped her shoulder with the end of the reins. Surprised, the little mare took off at a gallop that lengthened and flattened into a run.

"Don't stumble, Queenie, please don't," Hannah begged as they raced downhill. Near the bottom there was a place as steep as a shed roof. Hannah made Queenie walk there, but when they were down she urged her on again. She forgot she'd ever been scared she couldn't make Queenie move fast enough. She forgot about falling off, though by now the mare's back and sides were slippery with sweat. When she felt herself sliding she'd grab at Queenie's mane. The miles flew by under Queenie's hooves. Hannah tried to remember the directions Tamar had given her, but it didn't really matter. She had only to follow the hoofmarks and dung in the churned-up, dusty road.

They passed the Quaker woman's house and turned sharp left downhill. Somewhere soon they should come to the brook Tamar had told her about. Hannah couldn't see very far ahead because of the woods on each side and the curves in the road. She was going too fast to hear anything but the pound of Queenie's hooves.

Suddenly Queenie propped her legs under her and came to an abrupt stop. Hannah went over her head. She wasn't hurt, but it took a moment to gather her wits. She seemed to be sitting in about three inches of water with a couple of young steers, who were backing away from her in alarm.

"Hannah?" It was Jacob's voice.

Yes, she was sitting in shallow water and surrounded by cattle. They'd been drinking. Their mouths were still dribbling, and they looked surprised and rather reproachful. Both up and down stream were more cattle.

"Hannah, oh, Hannah!" Jacob looked as surprised as the steers, but he wasn't as polite. He was laughing. *Laughing!*

Hannah got up and squeezed water out of her skirts. "So you think it's funny," she said furiously. "You think it's funny to see a girl spilled when she's ridden hard all the way from Bedford to catch up with you. To tell you the Refugees aim to make off with your cattle. That you don't have much time to do anything about it."

"Hannah, what is this all about?" Mr. Isaacs had ridden up. He had a gun in front of his saddle and Queenie's reins looped over one arm.

"It's this, sir," Hannah said, turning her back on Jacob. "De Lancey was sent word last night about your taking cattle to Peekskill by way of Pine's Bridge."

"Who told you that?" Mr. Isaacs sounded short. He wasn't wasting any time laughing at her. And his hand touched his gun.

"I can't tell you, sir, I promised not."

"Hannah, I have to know if I'm to believe it."

"I know who it was, sir." Jacob took Queenie's reins from his father. "But if Hannah promised not to tell, I can't either. Believing won't hurt us any, though. And not believing could cost us the cattle."

He turned to Hannah, and he wasn't laughing now either. "How much time do we have, Hannah?"

"The man on Guard Hill hadn't seen any sign of mounted troops when I rode by. That's all I know. Except I rode faster than I've ever done before."

Jacob faced his father again. "If we run the cattle, there may still be time to get them across the bridge and take up the planks."

Mr. Isaacs pulled at his beard and thought. In less than a minute he'd made up his mind.

"Jon! Sam!" he called, and two men Hannah hadn't seen before answered. One was upstream and one down, behind the drinking cattle.

"Get the cattle out of the water and on the road," Mr. Isaacs shouted. "And get them running. Jacob, you stay here, and don't let them turn back toward Bedford."

Mr. Isaacs spurred his horse into the stream. Whips cracked, cattle bawled, and water splashed.

Jacob lifted Hannah up on Queenie and then mounted his own horse. "I'm sorry I laughed," he apologized. "It was the critters more than you. They looked so surprised."

"It's all right, Jacob," Hannah said. Maybe when there was time, she'd laugh about it, too.

As the cattle came out of the water, Jacob turned the ones that tried to head back. Hannah broke a sapling branch and made herself a switch.

"Go on home, Hannah," Jacob said once, but after that he seemed glad of her help. Queenie was handy, and whenever an animal left the road for the woods, Hannah rode after it. Then, when the strays were back in the water and headed the right way, she and Jacob went splashing into the stream, too. When the water came up to the horses' knees, Queenie put her head down to drink.

"Don't let her. She'll founder," Jacob called back as he splashed on ahead. Hannah pulled Queenie's head up and kicked her. In a minute she was following Jacob's horse up the west bank.

The cattle that hadn't strayed were some distance on, running with tails and rumps high and heads low, kicking up a storm of dust. Hannah heard Jon and Sam shouting, but she couldn't see them on account of the dust. She could hardly see Mr. Isaacs, who was just in front of her. She choked, and Jacob came up beside her and grabbed Tamar's kerchief from her head. "Tie it over your nose," he shouted. If it hadn't been already tied, Hannah couldn't have done it, but she managed to slip it into position without losing either reins or switch. Now that she could breathe again she was enjoying the run so much she almost forgot why they were running. Then through the dust straight ahead, over the backs of the cattle she saw a broad curve of water. The Croton! As they neared it, the woods fell away, and she could see the bridge and the road leading toward it from North Castle Church.

There were two small figures on the road close to the bridge. Men on horses. Even through the dust she could see that. Hannah was too excited to feel immediate fear, but then it came flooding through her. The men could be scouts for De Lancey, and the other men close behind. They'd take the cattle. Maybe they'd kill Jacob. She and Queenie hadn't done any good in coming.

Then she heard Mr. Isaacs say, "I'll go help Jon and Sam. Let the animals slow down if they will, Jacob." He rode to the left of the cattle, spurring his horse until he passed them.

"Whoaup," Jacob sang out, "whoaup, you critters."

It took a moment for Hannah to understand and pull Queenie in. The two horsemen were Mr. Isaacs' helpers. They had gone to block the road from North Castle Church and steer the cattle onto the bridge.

Gradually the cattle slowed to a lope, their rumps humping up and down and their necks held higher so she could see their horns. At first they didn't want to go over the bridge. They tried to scatter, and it took fast riding by Jon and Sam to keep them together and moving in the right direction. One or two tried to bolt into the river, but Mr. Isaacs was ready for them.

"If they turn, get out of the way fast," Jacob told Hannah, but the cattle didn't turn. With Jacob and Hannah behind them they moved steadily forward.

"Look!" Jacob pointed to the bridge. "That's the heifer we belled because she acted the leader while the cattle were fenced up back of the Raymonds'. There won't be any more trouble. Now she's on the bridge the others will follow."

They watched some others set foot on the bridge, too. Then Jacob said, "Good-bye, Hannah. You have helped more than there's time to say. Now go back. I don't want you around when the Refugees find the bridge is taken up."

"Jacob, when will I know that you got the cattle safe to Peekskill? That you are safe?"

"Don't worry if we're not back for a while. We will lay up for a day in a safe place my father knows about. And then we'll take a roundabout route instead of the usual one. It will take longer."

Jacob rode over the bridge behind the last of the cattle. The men dismounted and took up the planks one by one and carried them to the far shore.

Hannah waved good-bye to Jacob, and he waved back. At first in a friendly way and then gesturing as though he were impatient. Of course, it was too far to be sure, but it looked like that. She turned Queenie and rode slowly away. When they passed the first turn, she slipped from the horse's back.

"Oh, Queenie, you were good, real good!" she said, stroking the lathered neck. "We are going to walk all the way home to Bedford, and I'll lead you as far as the brook. If you're not cool enough when we come to it, we'll wait until you are, so you can have a nice long drink."

CHAPTER 16

Queenie was in the brook, her muzzle deep in water, when Hannah heard the first shot. Instinctively she jerked the mare's head up. There was a second shot from the west, hard on the first, and then silence. Hannah had seen the planks of the bridge lifted and the Isaacs' safe on the other side, but there was something happening she didn't understand. She only knew it must have something to do with De Lancey's Refugees.

She led Queenie out of the water and onto the road, uncertain in her mind. The Isaacs' should be safe across the Croton, yet she was afraid for them. She couldn't go back to Bedford until she understood about the shooting. She stood still, listening, waiting.

In the woods a chickadee was calling *dee, dee, dee.* The brook was burbling over stones. At the side of the road some insect was making a high shrill noise. There were no more sounds of shooting. Of course the bridge was a mile away, but she'd heard the first shots. She'd hear more if they came.

Hannah's thoughts were so concentrated on the bridge that at first she paid no attention to a clop-clop coming from the other direction. Queenie pulled at the reins and faced back toward Bedford. Then Hannah turned, too. Around the bend tore a mule. Its rider was pounding its ribs with his heels and belaboring its rump with the ends of a pair of long driving reins. The rider, she saw with disbelief, was her brother, Elijah.

Queenie was standing sideways, blocking the road. The mule stopped short. Elijah hung on, but only because the mule threw up its head and pushed him back.

For a moment neither Hannah nor Elijah had words. They were too surprised at seeing each other. Then, breathing hard, Elijah cried out, "De Lancey's had word the Isaacs' are driving cattle. We have to catch up and warn them."

"You want to warn the Isaacs'? *You?*" The scorn in Hannah's voice didn't seem to reach Elijah.

"The meat's for the American army, Hannah. Don't you understand? If you won't help, just get out of my way." His legs came down with a thump on each side of the mule.

Hannah was almost tempted to let him go on. Right into the shooting if more should come. She didn't believe his good intentions for a minute.

"Who gave De Lancey the word?" she asked, taking hold of the mule's bridle. "Tell me that, Elijah."

"Elliott."

Hannah's eyes never left her brother's face, and her hand stayed tight clamped on the mule's bridle. "And who told Elliott?"

Suddenly Elijah's face crumpled. "It was me, Hannah. Me. Now won't you believe the drove is in danger? Won't you let me loose so I can warn the Isaacs'?"

Before Hannah could answer they both heard a horse coming at a gallop from the direction of Pine's Bridge. The rider reined in sharply when he came abreast of them.

"You young people had best get off the road," he said. "There's a party of De Lancey's Refugees down by the bridge, and they're mad as hornets. They will be coming this way soon."

Hannah looked up at the man and recognized the weaselly features of Ezra Hunter, the man people said spied for the British. The last time she'd seen him he was with Major Tallmadge, the day she'd written to Pa about the burning. Well, it didn't matter now whether he was a spy or not. She needed to ask a question. She wouldn't have to answer any.

"What happened, Mr. Hunter? I heard shooting. Down by the bridge."

"The planks were up. Some of the Refugees tried to swim their horses across the river. Those in the front got shot at from the other side. By a man driving cattle."

"Was—was anyone hurt?" Hannah was almost afraid to ask.

"No. Unless it's one of De Lancey's men, who was still in the water when I passed. I wasn't too close. Didn't want to get mixed up. And you'd better not either. Get your animals into the woods till the Refugees go by. They're coming this way."

Ezra Hunter put spurs to his horse and galloped off. Hannah hesitated. Now that she knew about the shooting, she longed to get back home. If Queenie were as fresh as Mr. Hunter's horse, it would be safe to risk a run. But Queenie wasn't fresh. It wouldn't be fair or safe to ask it of her. And the mule Elijah was riding was tired, too—its ribs were pumping in and out like bellows. The question of where the mule had come from slid into Hannah's mind and out. It wasn't important now. Already, faint in the distance but coming closer, she could hear the rhythmic pounding of hooves.

"Come on, Elijah," she cried, and plunged off the road, dragging Queenie with her. Elijah kicked the mule's sides, but the animal had had enough running. Elijah slid off and beat him in the rear with the long reins, but the mule only planted his feet more firmly.

"Leave him," Hannah urged as she shouldered a way

into the woods for herself and Queenie. Thorny underbrush grabbed at her skirts, and wild-grape vines tangled themselves around Queenie's legs and chest. They scrambled over fallen tree trunks and made their way around upended roots.

The Refugees were close now. Hannah could hear shouts as well as the thud of galloping hooves. She and Queenie were safely hidden, standing in a hole caused by the uprooting of a giant oak and sheltered behind a ten-foot spread of roots. But she had no idea of what had become of Elijah. She climbed up the side of the hole and peered through the roots. She could see part of the road, the part that crossed the brook. And there in the water stood Elijah, tugging at the mule's bridle and walloping his sides with the reins.

"Leave him, Elijah. *Leave him!*" The cry was in her throat, but already it was too late. About twenty horsemen came around the bend. The mule let out a bray and kicked his heels up sideways. The first horse shied, and the others stopped suddenly, nearly unseating their riders. One man cursed. Then another said, "That's a good strong mule, and rare in these parts. Let's take him."

Elijah's back was to Hannah now. She couldn't see his face. She didn't know how scared he'd be looking, but his voice was loud enough to carry.

"Please leave him, sir. I borrowed him to come and help you. I have to return him."

"Help us!" The man gave a jeering laugh and grabbed the mule's bridle. Elijah hung onto the reins and wouldn't let go. If the mule had been willing to move, Elijah would have been dragged off his feet. The man swore, the mule brayed, and an officer Hannah knew rode forward. Captain Roger Halstead, Tamar's uncle. He looked down at Elijah.

"It's the Mills lad," he said. "The one who told my brother about the drive. If my nephew, Elliott, had ridden faster, we'd have captured the cattle this side of the bridge. But we will have them anyway. So leave the mule. We don't want the boy in trouble on our account."

The man started to argue, but Captain Halstead cut him short. "As De Lancey isn't here, I'm in command. I say let the mule be. And the boy. Let's go on."

The troop began to splash through the brook, giving wide berth to the mule's heels. Elliott was among the last.

"Good-bye, Elijah," Hannah heard him say as he waited his turn. "I've joined the regiment now, so I won't be coming back to Bedford."

Then, as his horse entered the water, he called over his shoulder, "Sorry you won't see the fun. We are crossing the river farther north at Veal's Ford. We aim to capture the drove where the road from the ford meets the road from the bridge."

"Well, you won't," Hannah felt like shouting after his retreating figure. The drove wouldn't be on the road where they'd be waiting for it. It would be hidden safe as Jacob had said.

When the dust raised by the troop settled, and the sound of voices and hoofbeats faded into the distance, Hannah led Queenie out of the woods.

"It was brave of you to stay with the mule, Elijah," she said going up to him. "The Refugees mightn't have believed what you said about coming to help them. They could have thought you warned the Isaacs'. They could have strung you up on a tree."

"I thought of that." Elijah's voice was shaking. "I thought of it, but I couldn't leave him for the Refugees to take." His eyes were fixed on some pebbles at the bottom of the brook. "I didn't ask to borrow him. He was hitched to a harrow, but no one was around, so I just took him. If I didn't bring him back, it would be as bad as if I stole him."

Hannah swallowed the words that first came to her. "Go on, Elijah," she said.

"Oh, Hannah, I didn't know American soldiers were hungry. The dragoons always had enough, but these were just bones."

"Who, Elijah? What are you talking about?"

"Foot soldiers. There were about a dozen. Early this morning before anyone but me was around. I caught them taking eggs and vegetables. They were sucking the eggs raw out of the shells. They said they'd come from above Peekskill and were on their way home to Connecticut. They hadn't had proper rations for weeks. Not even bread, unless they stole it. They looked awful, Hannah. When they left, they said they felt mean about stealing from a burned-out village where folks mightn't have enough for themselves."

"What did you say to that?" Hannah couldn't help asking.

"Nothing." Elijah looked uncomfortable. Ashamed, too. Hannah let the subject be.

"I *had* to borrow the mule, Hannah." Elijah's eyes went back to the pebbles. "At first I just kept thinking about those soldiers and hoping they'd get home all right. Later I got thinking about the soldiers at Peekskill. About how they needed food and how I'd fixed it so the cattle wouldn't get there. I had to do something about it. I ran and ran on foot until I found the mule in a field at the Raymonds'. Then I made him run. It was no good, all that running. I started too late."

He sounded bitter. As though he hated himself, real hard. Hannah felt her feeling for him warming.

"Well, you tried, Elijah," she said. "That was good. You tried, and you stood up to the Refugees when I'd have been scared to. I guess I'm almost proud of you, Elijah."

"You *are*, Hannah?" Elijah's voice was unbelieving,

but hopeful. "Oh, Hannah. I thought no one could ever be. Never. I thought after I gave back the mule, I'd run away."

"You can't," Hannah said firmly. "We've got to build a house together. A place for Pa when he gets home. A place for us to live through the winter. We'd freeze in the shelter. We'd better get home and start planning. Right now."

Elijah hung back. "Hannah, I've got to tell you something else. I did some stealing, too. So I could buy a gun like Elliott's and join up somewhere. I'm big as some sixteen-year-olds, and I wanted to fight like Pa did. Only I put everything back where I found it."

Hannah looked at the ground, so Elijah couldn't see she already knew about the stealing.

"It was wrong to steal, but I'm glad you returned everything," she said. "Now let's go."

Hannah got on Queenie, and Elijah scrambled up on the mule. At first the animal refused to budge, but when Queenie started to leave him behind, he changed his mind.

Queenie had the faster walk. The mule ambled along behind except when Elijah kicked him into a jog when he wanted to ask a question.

"Hannah, what will the Refugees do to Jacob and Mr. Isaacs when they take the drove where Elliott said?"

"They won't." Hannah leaned forward and brushed a deerfly off Queenie's ear. "The drove is off the road and hidden. When it's safe, the Isaacs' will take it on to Peekskill. Jacob said so."

"You mean that, Hannah? That I didn't really fix things so the American soldiers wouldn't get it?"

Hannah nodded, and Elijah gave a great sigh of relief. He let the mule fall back, but a little later he thought of something else and came up beside Queenie again.

"You said Jacob, Hannah. Then you saw him. Was it you gave the warning?"

"Yes, Elijah," Hannah said and then added generously, "But only because Queenie is so much faster than the mule."

Elijah thought again. "Did Tamar lend you Queenie? Or did you borrow her the way I borrowed the mule?"

Hannah hesitated. But only a minute. He had to be trusted. "She lent her to me, but you must never tell. It would get Tamar and her mother into terrible trouble."

"I won't then," Elijah promised. "Tamar's my friend. It was Tamar who untied me right after the burning, when a Ranger had tied me up for sassing him."

"She's my friend, too, now." It made Hannah feel good to be able to say this.

The eight-mile journey back to Bedford was so slow at a walk that the sun was right above them when they reached Guard Hill. It was hot, too. Hannah halted at the top to let a breeze blow across her forehead and the back of her neck. As they went on, nearing the Raymond farm, Elijah kept close to her side.

"What'll I say when I give back the mule?" he asked. He looked so scared that Hannah wished she had an answer that would help. But she didn't.

"I don't know. But you have to keep the Halsteads—all of them—out of it, or Tamar will be hurt."

They rode on in silence until they could see the opening in the wall and the cattle tracks coming out onto the road from it.

"I'll say I took the mule to race," Elijah said as if relieved to have that settled.

"Likely you'll get a licking."

Unconsciously, Elijah slid a hand between himself and the mule. "I guess."

At the farm cartway they stopped.

"Well, I'd better get it over with." Elijah left her there to ride on to the farm buildings at the back alone.

CHAPTER 17

At the crossroads Hannah slid to the ground and slipped off Queenie's bridle. "Thank you, Queenie," she said, putting her cheek against the soft muzzle. Then she walked to the rear and gave the mare a slap on the rump. "Go on home now, and tell Tamar we got there in time."

Queenie trotted off, and Hannah laid the bridle on the ground where Tamar had told her. She gave a little sigh of relief. She hadn't met anyone except Jacob, who recognized Queenie, though it had been a close call with Elliott.

Without thinking, Hannah turned down toward the Common. And then she remembered. She had told Mrs. Slawson she was sick. She had asked her to keep Andrew and Liddy so she could go back to the shelter to rest. She couldn't just appear from the opposite direction without some explanation. It was a nuisance, but there was no help for it. She'd have to circle around by way of Indian Hill. She'd better wash some of the dust off, too, while she was there. A girl wouldn't get that dirty just lying quiet.

Climbing down the cliff from the high meadow, Hannah was feeling elated. Everything had gone just the way it should. She'd caught up with the Isaacs' in time, and the Refugees had missed out on capturing the drove. They would wait and wait on the other side of the Croton for the cattle that would never show up where they expected. The wet hem of her skirt brushed against her ankle, and suddenly she began to laugh. Jacob was right. Those steers had looked surprised when she landed in the brook with them.

Hannah was still laughing when she reached the shelter. Then abruptly laughter turned to anger. Eben Baylor was inside, poking around Ma's things. The open needle case was in his hands.

"Give me that!" Hannah cried. "You have no right to touch that."

"What's the harm?" Eben asked insolently as he gave it to her. "I wouldn't have taken the money. I was just passing time waiting for you."

"Well, it's too bad a girl can't go to the bushes for a minute without you prying into what's none of your business."

"A minute!" Eben leered. "That was a good long trip to the bushes. I've been here more than an hour. Ever since Mrs. Slawson sent me for you when Liddy fell out of the tree."

Liddy! Heart in throat, Hannah raced out to the road and then down it. If Liddy was bad hurt, she didn't want to hear it from Eben. She pictured her little sister lying on the ground in a heap and not moving. She pictured the blue eyes closed and the honey-colored hair spread out around a white, white face. "Oh, Liddy," she begged, "please be all right."

Her breath came shorter and shorter as she ran, but at last she turned into the Slawsons' lot. Andrew ran up to her. "Oh, Hannah, Liddy cried and cried for you. Where were you?"

"Andrew, how is she?" Hannah looked around wildly. "What have they done with her?"

"Mrs. Baylor took her."

"She's all right, Hannah." Mrs. Slawson joined them. "Had the wind knocked out when she fell from the tree. More scared than hurt."

"She didn't want to go with Mrs. Baylor." Andrew's face was stormy. "I kicked Mrs. Baylor. I kicked and kicked her when she took Liddy. But she wouldn't set her down."

"Oh, Andrew, you shouldn't have," Hannah said.

"You will find Liddy at the Baylors' shelter," Mrs. Slawson told her. Her face, usually so kind, looked tight-lipped and disapproving. "We sent Eben to fetch you. When you didn't come, we knew you weren't where you said. You had no need to lie to me, Hannah."

"Oh, ma'am, I didn't want to!" Hannah cried, but Mrs. Slawson turned away.

At the Baylors' shelter Liddy was lying on a blanket sniffling, a big bump on her forehead. Mrs. Baylor was stirring something over the fire. They both saw Hannah at the same time. Liddy stretched out her arms and began to sob.

"Take me home, Hannah, I want to go home!"

"Of course, lovey." Hannah ran and knelt beside her, gathering her close. "Where do you hurt?"

"She's not hurt anywhere except for that bump," Mrs. Baylor said grimly. "But you're not taking her home either. I wouldn't feel right letting you. Running off today, heaven knows where. And last night, too."

Hannah felt as though part of the cliff had fallen on her. Her brain refused to work. She had no answer, except to hold Liddy closer.

"I don't know what your Ma would think of such goings-on." Mrs. Baylor took the pan off the fire and thumped it down on a stone. "Maybe it's best she's underground."

"Don't you say that." Hannah found her tongue. "Don't you dare! I've done nothing to shame Ma. Come on, Liddy. We're going home." She helped the child to her feet.

"Not till you explain, miss." Mrs. Baylor stood in front of them, arms folded.

"I don't have to. Not to you. Ma left me in charge of the young ones. I'm responsible to Ma and Pa. Not to anyone else." Hannah was trembling all over. What would she do if Mrs. Baylor tried to keep Liddy by force?

But Mrs. Baylor stepped aside. "We'll see about that," she sniffed.

It was easy to soothe Liddy once they were back at their own shelter. Hannah soaked a cloth in cold water from the stream and laid it on her forehead.

"I won't leave you again," she promised, "but last night I had to. And today. I feel worse than you that I wasn't here when you fell. Were you scared?"

Liddy nodded. "I was scared when you didn't come. But I wasn't scared last night when I woke because Andrew said you'd be back soon. Hannah, can I have a piece of the cake Rachel sent? I'm hungry."

The cake was where Hannah had left it covered, but one whole corner was gone. *Eben,* she thought angrily as she cut off a slice.

"Liddy," she asked, taking it to her, "how did Mrs. Baylor know about last night?"

"I told her." The little girl put a morsel in her mouth and licked her fingers afterward. "She asked if you'd ever left me before. I had to tell her the truth, didn't I, Hannah?" A small worried frown showed as she let the cloth slip from her forehead.

"Yes, you did." Hannah put a comforting arm around her. "Ma didn't hold with lying. We have to do the way she taught us. I promised we would."

Hannah wondered what Ma would think of the lying she'd done to Mrs. Slawson. Ma would have found some other way, she was sure. Maybe she wouldn't have given any reasons at all. Hannah sighed. Now Mrs. Slawson thought badly of her, and she'd made an enemy of Mrs. Baylor. It was worrisome, but there was no use in letting it worry Liddy.

Bringing Magnolia with them, Elijah and Andrew came back from the village together.

"I saw Tamar," Elijah said. "She was by the crossroads, and she had Queenie's bridle. I told her what happened."

"What happened?" Andrew wanted to know.

A story started forming in Hannah's mind, but she rejected it. "We can't tell anyone, Andrew. Please don't ask."

"But Elijah told Tamar," Andrew protested, his face puckering.

"Please tell. Please!" Liddy begged, but Elijah refused.

Long after Andrew and Liddy were asleep that evening, Hannah and Elijah stayed up and talked about building. With a stick, Elijah marked out the shape of the cellar in the dirt by the fireplace.

"We will need four big beams for sills," he said, drawing them. "Then about eight crossbeams and long boards going the other way on top."

"That's more wood than I counted on needing," Hannah said. "It will cost a lot of money."

"I know it will," Elijah agreed. "But I know how much we have to have because of watching Pa build. I carried tools for him from the time I could walk."

"Yes, you did, Elijah." Hannah's eyes were on the drawing. Then, as though she'd decided something, she raised them. "I should have remembered you'd know more than me about building. I should have asked you in the first place, not just said what we were going to do."

Elijah looked a little embarrassed. It was a new way for Hannah to be talking. "It doesn't matter, anyway, if we don't have the money for it," he said gruffly.

"We have the money in the needle case," Hannah reminded him. "Maybe it's enough for the two long sill beams. You can ask Mr. Slawson tomorrow. It would be a start."

Elijah's face brightened. "I could start cutting the notches in the sills for the floor beams to rest in. I guess Pa will be surprised when he gets home and finds how much I know about carpentering."

Hannah's eyes filled with sudden tears, but they didn't spill over. "Pa may never get home," she said. "He was near starved when he wrote last time. Ma only read us the good parts. The letter's in the Bible. You're old enough to read it, Elijah."

Hannah got up early and mixed johnnycake from the cornmeal Mr. Isaacs had brought. She heaped coals on the lid of the iron kettle to bake it and then milked Magnolia. Now all the Isaacs' were away, there was milk to spare. She'd set some aside to sour and make cheese, she decided. Butter, too. Ma had always made butter and cheese when they had more milk than they needed themselves. Sometimes Ma sold it, and sometimes she traded. Hannah wondered if Mr. Slawson might be willing to take some in trade for wood. Elijah could ask that, too.

After breakfast Elijah took Magnolia to the Common. Later, Hannah followed him down to the village with Andrew and Liddy. She set them to sorting bricks, then went next door. She had to make things right with Mrs. Slawson.

"I'm sorry I lied to you yesterday," she told her. "I had no call to."

"No, you didn't," Mrs. Slawson agreed, but she

looked friendly again. "But I'm sorry now I let out what you said about needing to go back and rest."

"It doesn't matter, ma'am, so long as you forgive me."

"I hope not." Mrs. Slawson looked troubled. "But Mrs. Baylor's making something of the lie. She's a good Christian woman, Hannah, but hard to stand against. I couldn't keep her from taking Liddy when she fell. She blamed me for letting her up in the tree."

Hannah did, too, but there was no sense in making Mrs. Slawson feel bad.

"She wasn't hurt any," she said. "Ma'am—Elijah was going to ask Mr. Slawson if we could buy some sawed wood to start rebuilding."

Mrs. Slawson nodded. "Yes, he came by. Mr. Slawson is at the mill, so I sent him on." A quick pleased look came into the woman's eyes. "Have you heard your father is being exchanged? Is that why you're wanting wood right now? After all these months in prison, I'm sure Mr. Slawson will be glad to credit him for what he needs until he can pay."

It was a temptation to let Mrs. Slawson believe Pa was coming home, but Hannah shook her head. "No, ma'am, that's not it. We haven't heard from Pa since April. It's Elijah and me that's going to do the building. We have to have a place for the winter. For me and Elijah and the young ones and Magnolia."

Mrs. Slawson put an arm around Hannah. "Child, it's good you cleaned the place up, but it's no use for you to build. Not even if you were able. Not unless your father gets home."

"Why not?" Hannah's body stiffened.

"Because Mrs. Baylor has set her mind against you children living by yourselves any longer."

Mrs. Slawson sounded as though there were nothing to do except what Mrs. Baylor decided. Hannah was angry that a grown woman could be so spineless.

"Mrs. Baylor has no right to go against what I promised Ma," she shouted. "She has no rights over us at all. I'm not scared of her. Elijah and I are going to build us a place. If Mr. Slawson won't sell us sawed wood, we will make do with what we can chop."

Mrs. Slawson looked hurt. "It's not a matter of wood, Hannah."

Immediately Hannah was contrite. "I'm sorry for what I said about the wood. It was no way to talk to a person who's been so good to us. Ma would be ashamed of me."

"She'd understand, Hannah. So do I. It was your father's spunk talking." She dabbed at her eyes with a corner of her apron. "I think your mother would be real proud of you, Hannah. But from where she is now, I'm not sure she'd want to hold you to any promise."

CHAPTER 18

In the early afternoon Mr. Slawson and Elijah brought a load of lumber over from the mill by oxcart. Most of it was for the Slawsons, but there were two long beams for the Mills'. Mr. Slawson helped Elijah set them on each side of the cellar and then sat down on one. Refusing the money Hannah held out, he said, "I'll credit what lumber you need."

Hannah felt a warm rush of gratitude, but she had to be sure. "Didn't Elijah tell you Pa may not be home to do the building?"

"Yes, he did." Mr. Slawson took off his hat and fanned himself with it. "But he explained how you plan to use the wood. I guess you young people can do that much alone if I give a hand with the lifting. The rest can wait till your father gets back."

"But if Pa never gets back? It's the credit I'm thinking of." It was hard to have to put it that plain.

Mr. Slawson smiled. "It's not your pa I'm crediting, Hannah. It's Elijah. Next week he's starting work at the mill. With people beginning to rebuild, there will be more work than my brother and I can handle. A smart twelve-year-old will be a lot of help."

Twelve-year-old! Well, Elijah was near enough that, for Hannah to let it pass.

"I helped with some boards this morning, and Mr.

Slawson said I did real good." Elijah was swishing flies away from the oxen and looked proud enough to bust. "I'll work here evenings."

Hannah nodded agreement. It would put more on her shoulders again, but he'd found a way to be important. Really important. She wouldn't have kept him from it if she could.

Several times that afternoon Hannah saw Mrs. Baylor looking over at the beams. She must know what they were planning, but she was holding her tongue. Well, Mrs. Baylor wasn't so hard to stand up against as Mrs. Slawson thought. Hannah remembered how she'd stepped aside yesterday to let her take Liddy home. And now she was minding her own business. Mrs. Baylor was mean and bossy, but it seemed all that was needed to stand against her was spine.

Elijah drove the ox team back to the mill, so he didn't start work on the beams that day. During the night it began to rain. Not thunder-and-lightning rain, but steady rain that didn't let up. It dripped between the saplings that made the front part of the shelter. Only the back part beneath projecting rock was really dry. Elijah and Andrew moved their blankets under cover and brought in wood to keep the fire alive. It was cozy, Hannah thought, to be shut away from the village and living so close together.

All the next day, while Andrew made up games to amuse himself and Liddy, Elijah spent hours on the dirt floor drawing more plans. Hannah watched as he drew the base of the big central chimney with its cellar oven that Ma had often used for extra baking.

"The oven will do for a fireplace till Pa gets back," he said. "Some bricks fell down inside from the top of the chimney, but I cleared them out. The flue works fine."

Though he'd read the letter in the Bible, Elijah always said "when" or "till Pa gets back." Never the "if" that sometimes escaped Hannah's lips.

"Oh, Elijah, the cellar is going to be almost as comfortable as a real house!" she exclaimed. "Pa will be proud of how well you've planned."

Elijah looked pleased and went on drawing. At the end where there were high-up windows because of the slope of the land, he drew a table and some benches. At the other end, a stall and some bins.

The second morning it was still raining. The boys got wet doing outside chores. When he came in, Elijah put on dry trousers and began a new drawing. He said it was going to be a low slanting roof of saplings and sod to keep rain and snow off the sawed boards. Hannah didn't notice when this drawing was finished and he went to Pa's tool box in the corner. And she only half heard something drop because her mind was on Ma. She was sewing up a rip in Andrew's smock and remembering when Ma had made it from an old dress of Grandma Mills'. Sometime, she knew, she'd have to start using Ma's clothes, but they were still too much a part of Ma to cut up.

"Hannah!" There was something strange in Elijah's voice. Jerked out of her thoughts, she looked up quickly, afraid he'd hurt himself.

"Hannah, I've found it." The tone was one of disbelief. Then it changed to a shout. "The money! It's here! Come and see!"

The floor around the tool box was covered with nails. But not just nails. There were coins, too. And paper money.

"I dropped the nail sack when I was looking for Pa's chisels. The nails spilled out, and then the money," Elijah explained. He was on his knees, separating money from nails. Hannah and Andrew and Liddy threw themselves down beside him.

"We're rich. We're rich!" Andrew chanted happily as Hannah started to count the money.

"Rich," Liddy repeated after him. Suddenly she stood up and threw a handful of paper money into the air.

"No, Liddy, no!" Hannah screamed, but she wasn't really angry. It was lovely to feel rich. A hundred dollars in Continental paper and ten pounds in hard money wasn't a fortune, but it seemed so when they'd been so near destitute.

Impulsively she took four pennies from the pile they'd counted. "These are for us," she said. "To spend on anything we want."

"I'll keep mine with my treasures," Liddy decided.

Elijah and Andrew put theirs in holes in the rock wall. "For when there's a store again," Andrew said.

Hannah put hers in Ma's work basket. "I should have looked under the nails long ago," she said, "only it wasn't like Ma to hide things from us. I forgot she'd expect the Hessians might search what we took out of the house and would hide the money from them."

"Well, we have it now." Elijah was jubilant. "Oh, Hannah, it means we can buy glass for the windows! I wasn't sure we could."

It would mean they had enough for all the things they really needed so they could stay together, Hannah thought with satisfaction. When winter came, they would have shoes, and she could buy wool already spun to knit stockings and mittens and coverings for their heads. There would be enough for salt and flour and for pork at hog-killing time. With what they'd grown it would be more than enough. There'd be no reason for anyone to think they couldn't get along all right by themselves.

It stopped raining during the night, and the sun came out on a fresh clean world from which the dust of two weeks had been washed away. The bushes near the shelter were fairly asking for someone to spread clean clothes on them to dry.

Elijah filled the wash kettle and built up the fire before he left for the village to work on the beams. Hannah put soap and clothes in the kettle and then started tidying up the shelter. She sang as she worked. All the joyous hymns she could remember. On such a beautiful day, she couldn't help feeling that everything would be all right with Pa, too. He'd get the letter she'd given to Jacob. He'd ask for parole. He'd be allowed to come home and see them.

Every bush was covered with a shirt or trousers, a dress or an apron before Hannah was finally ready to start to the village herself. Andrew had Magnolia by the halter, and Liddy held a pan of scraps for the chickens.

"Come on, Hannah," Andrew was urging when Liddy piped up, "It's the pastor! He's stopping!"

The pastor had moved outside the village after the burning, and except for Sabbath meeting they hadn't seen him since he'd buried Ma. Hannah was happy to see him now and ran toward him, smiling.

"It's good of you to stop," she said in Ma's own words of greeting.

There was no answering smile on the long, rather sheeplike face. He spoke absently to the young ones, putting a hand on the head of each. Then he said, "Send them off, please, Hannah."

"Off?" Hannah was puzzled. She'd thought he'd stopped to pray with them as he had when Ma was alive. They had a lot to be thankful for today. She'd hoped he'd get down on his knees with them to give God thanks. But it seemed that wasn't why he'd come, or he'd want Andrew and Liddy to stay.

"Off?" she repeated.

"Yes. Mrs. Baylor is waiting for them at her shelter."

"I won't go," Andrew said flatly.

"I don't like Mrs. Baylor." Liddy began to cry. "Don't make me go. Please, Hannah."

"Nonsense, Lydia." The pastor used her given name sternly. "Mrs. Baylor loves you, and I have to talk to your sister alone."

Was it about Pa? Hannah wondered in sudden panic. Had the pastor been sent word Pa was dead?

"I'll kick her like I did before if I have to go," Andrew threatened.

"Please, Andrew. Please, Liddy. Do as the pastor wants," Hannah said, taking hold of Magnolia. Then, as they left, still protesting, she turned back to the pastor. "Is it about Pa, sir?"

"No, Hannah." The old man spoke sorrowfully. "It's about you. Complaints have been made about you to the elders and myself."

The words were so unexpected that Hannah couldn't believe she'd heard right. Complained of to the church? It couldn't be she he was talking about.

But it was. She could tell that by his face as he looked at her silently. What had she done? She'd lied to Mrs. Slawson, but surely it couldn't be that. Mrs. Slawson wouldn't have complained—no, but she'd said—yes, that must be it. She'd said Mrs. Baylor was making something of the lie!

"Was it Mrs. Baylor who did the complaining?" Hannah asked bitterly. "Well, she had no cause. I've already asked God to forgive me, and Mrs. Slawson, too."

"It was her duty to bring her complaints to the church," the pastor reproved. "It is the duty of every member to watch over his fellow members. I feel greatly to blame that I didn't watch over you more tenderly myself after your dear mother died."

If he had, maybe he'd have helped with Elijah when she was near frantic, Hannah thought. But that was over and done with now, and no sense in bringing it up.

"Ma taught us it's a sin to lie," she said. "I confess to that, but I've done nothing else wrong."

"That is for the church to decide," the pastor told her. "The elders have set a special session for Thursday evening. At that time they will listen to Mrs. Baylor's complaints and hear what you have to say."

Suddenly Hannah felt frightened. Who knew what Mrs. Baylor might make up about her? Discipline by the church could mean anything from a public confession at meeting to excommunication.

"I've done nothing wrong," she repeated but not as confidently now. "What does Mrs. Baylor say I've done?"

The pastor came so close she could smell his breath, and his voice became the exhorting one he used for preaching. "She complains you have violated the rules of the Gospel and behaved in such a way as to wound our Lord."

"It's not true!" Hannah cried; only it was more of a whisper. Feeling sick and dizzy, she leaned against Magnolia for support. The cow swung her head around and licked Hannah's arm. The warm, rough tongue brought tears. Hannah turned and buried her face in Magnolia's shoulder.

Behind her the pastor went on speaking. "Mrs. Baylor has asked that the church take you children into its loving care and find homes for you with God-fearing families. She is willing to take Liddy herself."

CHAPTER 19

For a long time after the pastor left her, Hannah stayed where he'd left her on her knees. At least that was where her body stayed, though it seemed more as if it belonged to someone else. That someone had prayed with the pastor, repeating words after him. Meaningless words that had nothing to do with her, Hannah Mills.

After a while she heard something moving in the bushes and looked up. Magnolia had Liddy's Sabbath dress over one horn like a lopsided bonnet. She'd have to get up and rescue it, but first she said a prayer in her own words.

"Please, God, help me do what is right for the young ones and me and Elijah. Please let us stay together."

She would have liked to go up on the top of Indian Hill and be alone until she felt in one piece again, but already it was too late. She saw Andrew and Liddy coming back from the Baylors'. They'd want to know what the pastor said and why they'd been sent away. There wasn't time, now, to think of herself. She had to decide what to tell them.

Andrew's underlip was jutting out the way it did when he was mad. Liddy's face was streaked with tears. They were still running down her cheeks.

"Hannah," she sobbed, "she called me her little girl. Are we going to give me away like we did Amy?"

Hannah felt as if a giant hand were squeezing her heart and wouldn't let go. It wasn't the sort of question she'd expected. What could she say? How could she tell Liddy no when actually the elders might send her to the Baylors till Pa got home?

"We didn't give Amy away," she said. That at least was true. "She's still ours, even if she's not living with us right now."

Then she added slowly, thinking it out as she spoke, "No matter where any of us live, we are still ours."

"Oh." Liddy stopped crying and smiled, tears still caught in her lashes. "I'm glad we didn't give me to Mrs. Baylor."

Hannah sighed. Liddy hadn't understood what she was trying to say, but she didn't have the heart to make things plainer right now. And just maybe there wouldn't be a need to.

"Let's feel the clothes and put the dry ones away," she suggested. Then, to avoid an angry outburst by Andrew, she asked him to take Magnolia to the Common. "But come right back," she told him. "We have things to do around the shelter today."

If there was already gossip in the village, she couldn't face it yet, and she didn't want Liddy and Andrew to hear it. She was surprised to find her hands and part of her mind could attend to everyday things like folding clothes while her heart and the rest of her mind were so sore and confused.

How had she violated the rules of the Gospel? How had she wounded the Lord? The pastor hadn't said, and she'd been too stunned to ask him. But just the accusations made her feel ashamed.

When Andrew came back, she sent both children into the woods. "I need some twigs for a new broom," she told them. "The old one's no use anymore. See what you can find."

Liddy and Andrew had only been gone about five minutes when a farm wagon stopped on the road opposite the shelter. A boy was driving it. There was a girl beside him. She looked like— Yes, it was—

"Rachel!" Hannah cried.

"Hannah!" Rachel cried at the same moment. She jumped down over the wheel, and the girls were in each other's arms. Then the boy got out, and Rachel introduced him as Silas Avery. She looked so proud that Hannah knew it must be the boy she'd written about in her letter. He'd come in to do some business for his father, he said, and brought Rachel along.

Rachel had a lot to say. It was nice living on the farm, she said, looking up at Silas coyly. Amy and Ben were both doing fine. Aaron missed Andrew. She'd been to a quilting frolic. One day last week Lieutenant Smith and Lieutenant O'Malley had passed the farm. They had asked about Hannah. Did Hannah remember the good times they'd had when Moylan was in Bedford?

Rachel looked so happy and pretty and Hannah was so glad to see her that she tried to respond whenever Rachel paused to draw her into the conversation. But the more Rachel chattered, the more she felt herself estranged from the life Rachel was rattling on about. It was as though she and Rachel were looking at each other from different worlds.

After a few minutes Silas said he'd have to be seeing to his father's business and he'd come by for Rachel later. When he'd gone, Rachel stopped her light chatter and turned on Hannah accusingly.

"Here I've been telling Silas that you're my best friend and what fun we'd all have together when he met you and now you had to act as if the cat had your tongue. Couldn't you be polite anyway? Don't you like him? Was that what ailed you?"

"Oh, no, Rachel! I do like him. Truly I do. But something just happened." Then she was pouring out the whole story. Rachel threw her arms around her, and Hannah could feel Rachel's tears on her own cheeks. They were close friends again.

"I'm so ashamed! Just thinking of me and all the fun I've been having," Rachel said. "Oh, Hannah, it's awful. What are you going to do?"

"I don't know," Hannah replied. "I haven't had time to think it out. I'm scared."

"Come home with me," Rachel suggested. "Don't go to that old session. No one can make you."

"I have to, Rachel. It's the *church*." Hannah didn't want to go either, but she was shocked by the idea. "And anyway if I didn't go, the elders would believe whatever Mrs. Baylor says."

"Do the others know? Elijah and Andrew and Liddy?"

"I'll tell Elijah. I want to keep the young ones from hearing till it's over if I can."

"They are sure to hear. No, wait. Not if I take them back to the farm."

"Could you, Rachel? Could you really?"

"Why not? Andrew can sleep in the bed with Aaron, and Liddy with me. There's lots of room. Mama suggested my bringing Andrew anyway."

"I'll get them then!"

They weren't far off and came running when Hannah called. Andrew was eager to go, but Liddy had to be persuaded.

"It's just a visit," Hannah told her. "A visit to see Amy. You won't be staying long."

"As long as Amy?" Liddy sounded dubious.

"No, not that long."

Liddy thought this over, and then she asked, "Can I take her a penny? So she'll know she's one of ours?"

"If you don't let her swallow it," Hannah agreed.

When Silas Avery returned to pick up Rachel, both the children had bundles of clothes ready, and Liddy was looking forward to a kitten, as well as seeing Amy. Until they were safe in the wagon and Silas touched the horses with his whip, Hannah was jumpy with nerves. What would she do if Mrs. Baylor happened by and tried to stop them? She cut her good-byes as short as she could even with Rachel, who clung to her.

"Hannah, you are so all alone. Is there no one to help?"

"Mrs. Slawson maybe. And Mr. Slawson."

"I wish Jacob was back."

So did Hannah. As the wagon rattled off down the road, she felt both relief and sudden terrible loneliness. She needed someone strong to hold fast to. She needed Jacob.

Until Elijah came back with Magnolia at suppertime, Hannah stayed inside the shelter. Then, while he milked and she fried eggs in the iron skillet, she told him about the pastor's visit and about sending the young ones to the Isaacs'. His face darkened, and Hannah could feel the anger rising up in him before it burst out.

"She has no right! What does she mean? I'll tell her to leave us alone. The snouty old sow." Elijah picked up a handful of stones and hurled them in the direction of the Baylors' shelter, shouting, "Sow, bug-tit, piss-cat, poop-head!"

Being caught in Elijah's anger was like being caught in a storm. But as long as it wasn't turned against her, Hannah just braced herself and waited for it to be over. She hadn't known Elijah knew so many bad words. In the end she persuaded him against going right over and repeating them to Mrs. Baylor.

"I don't know what all she has against me," she told

him, "but if you let out just one of those words, she'd find a way for blaming me."

"All right then, but I'll show her what I think of her trying to send me to live somewhere else. I'll finish the house this week before I start work at the mill. You will have to help."

"I will, Elijah." Hannah dreaded going down to the village, but she also felt the importance of finishing the house. Not to show Mrs. Baylor, but as an act of faith. To show God they trusted in Him.

In the morning as Hannah was starting out to help Elijah work on the house, Tamar stopped by. She walked up to the shelter openly and didn't seem to care who saw her.

"I've come to tell you that I am leaving Bedford," she said. "I'm glad to be friends again before I have to go."

"You are going, Tamar? Why?" For the moment Hannah forgot her own troubled thoughts. Had Tamar's father found out about the loan of Queenie? Was he sending her away as punishment?

"I never told anyone that you sent me to warn the Isaacs'," she said. "And I thought the only person who recognized Queenie was Jacob. He'd never tell."

"It hasn't anything to do with Queenie and you. Father was warned to get below British lines and stay there. He's in New York City now. Mother and I are waiting for passes to join him with our things."

"Oh, Tamar, what happened?"

"Mr. Hunter informed against him."

"But he's a spy for the British!"

"No. We only thought so. He'd been watching us to find out if Father was keeping neutral or giving aid to the British. Well, he found out." Tamar gave a bitter little laugh. "We aren't welcome in Bedford anymore."

"But you and your mother aren't Tories," Hannah protested. "You told me so. It isn't fair."

"No, but we have to go just the same. Don't worry about us, Hannah. We will be well treated in New York."

"I'm sorry I was mean so long. Can I ask you a favor, Tamar?"

"Of course."

"If you can, will you find out if Pa is still alive and let me know? He's in the Sugar House."

"I'll try, Hannah."

When Hannah finally went down to the village, she turned her head away as she passed the Baylors' lot. Mrs. Baylor didn't call out to her the way she usually did, but Hannah felt her watching as she and Elijah worked. Elijah had finished most of the square notches for the crossbeams to fit into when their ends were shaped and Mr. Slawson had delivered the rest of the wood. Elijah was showing Hannah how to chisel the ends of the joists when Mrs. Slawson left her children and came over.

"Hannah, I've heard," she said. "I hope the elders won't be hard on you, but Mrs. Baylor stands high with the pastor. She complained of us last year because we neglected morning prayers in our home. I've been timid around her ever since."

Suddenly appalled, Hannah put down the chisel and looked up into the woman's kind, distressed face.

"Oh, ma'am, I've neglected them, too. Ever since Ma died. I have prayed and heard the young ones' prayers at night, but that's all." Overcome with guilt, she wondered if that had wounded the Lord. If that was what the pastor had meant. She asked Mrs. Slawson.

"It could be that," Mrs. Slawson replied, shaking her head. "And of course, lying violates the rules of the Gospel. If those are Mrs. Baylor's complaints, you will have to make a public confession as we did, and that will end it. It's humiliating but deserved."

"But she's asked the church to put us in different homes!"

"That may not have anything to do with her complaints. She's thought all along you were too young to manage. I've watched you wearing yourself out and thought so myself at times. Elijah tells me you have sent Andrew and Liddy off for a visit. At least that will be a help while you have the extra work of building."

"That's not why I sent them!" Hannah exclaimed. "It's so they won't hear things against me. I'm not tired. I'm not!"

Every time she walked along the Street Hannah was conscious that people were talking about her, but nothing unkind was said. They looked at her, though, the way they'd looked when Ma was dying and they thought she didn't know.

By Thursday afternoon Hannah was so sick with worry she couldn't think of anything except the session. She'd confess to anything she'd done that was wrong. She'd do it there or openly at meeting. She'd not mind the humiliation so long as they let her keep the children.

The chisel slipped and cut more wood than she meant. When Elijah said something about it, she burst into tears and ran up the road toward the shelter.

CHAPTER 20

A man was coming toward her, but Hannah's eyes were too blurred with tears to see who it was. It wasn't until he took her into his arms and she was crying against his long beard that she knew it was Mr. Isaacs.

When she finished crying, he told her he'd returned from Peekskill the night before and spent it at the farm.

"Rachel is worried about you, Hannah. She says you are in trouble and that's why she brought Andrew and Liddy to visit. Her story seems incredible. Surely she can't have it right? Tell me yourself, child."

Still holding her, he listened gravely, shaking his head now and then.

"Do you know what specific accusations Mrs. Baylor is making against you?" he asked.

Hannah wiped her eyes on the lapels of his coat. "I think it's lying and neglecting morning prayers. It's all I can think of, sir."

Mr. Isaacs relaxed his hold a little. "I don't believe it's enough to warrant separating you children, but the session may be unpleasant. Would you like me to take you there and wait to bring you back?"

"Oh, sir, I would! I won't be so scared then."

"You realize I can't be with you at the session?"

"I know. It's between the church and me. But it will help to know you'll be waiting when it's over."

At six o'clock Mr. Isaacs called for Hannah, and she climbed up behind him on his horse.

"I wish I was going," Elijah said. "I'd like a chance to tell the elders what I think of that old—" Luckily the rest was lost as the horse moved forward.

They rode slowly through the village. People had already left off work, and the sound of saws and hammers had ceased, but Mr. Isaacs was interested in seeing how much had been done since he'd left for Peekskill. They stopped briefly to inspect the progress at the tavern. As they went on, Mr. Isaacs said, "Jacob will be home in a day or two. Then we will get busy again on our house."

"Did he find anyone to take my letter to Pa?" she asked.

"He will, Hannah, I'm sure of that."

The house where the pastor boarded was close to the Raymond farm. As they neared it, Hannah's arms tightened around Mr. Isaacs' waist. She didn't want the journey ended. She didn't want to face the pastor and the elders. Not yet. When the horse stopped, she slid off and waited, stiff with fear, while Mr. Isaacs tied it in a shed behind the house. Then they walked around front and he knocked at the door. As it swung open, she looked beyond the pastor at five men seated at a long table in front of the fireplace. From their gestures they seemed to be talking of building. Mrs. Baylor wasn't with them.

The pastor beckoned her in. Then, as Mr. Isaacs continued to stand on the doorstep, he said courteously, "Mr. Isaacs, you are a respected member of our community, but you are not of this congregation, so you will excuse me if I don't invite you in."

"I understand," Mr. Isaacs replied. "But Hannah is like a daughter to me. She is young to be out alone at night. Perhaps you will allow me to wait in some small room so I may escort her home when the session is ended?"

The pastor hesitated, but only for a moment. "You are welcome to do that, sir," he said. He opened a door to the left of the fireplace, and Mr. Isaacs passed through.

Though only a door separated them, Hannah felt abandoned. Whatever happened now, she would have to face alone. One of the elders, Mr. Seeley, looked up and nodded toward a chair. "Be seated, Hannah," he said. After that, no one spoke to her. They were talking about building a new meetinghouse. Hannah tried to think about that, but she couldn't keep her mind on it. She sat, twisting her hands in her lap and wondering what was going to happen to her.

Then there was a loud knock on the door, and Mrs. Baylor entered. Hannah glanced at the floor. She wished she were thin enough to slip down between the cracks.

"We will now commence with a prayer," the pastor said, and they all knelt. It was a prayer asking for forgiveness. Hannah repeated the words with the others. She wanted forgiveness for her lie and for neglecting morning prayers, but she knew she'd never forgive Mrs. Baylor.

When they rose from their knees, Mr. Seeley said, "As moderator of this session I suggest we take up the complaints of Mrs. Baylor before we discuss building plans. Mrs. Baylor, I understand you have allegations to make against Hannah Mills, a sister in this church?"

"Yes. It is my sad duty to complain of her." Mrs. Baylor sounded so truly sorry that Hannah wondered if after all she would be kind. But then she went on, "Our sister has violated the—"

"Let us have it more plainly, Mrs. Baylor. It is for us to decide about violations," the moderator cut her short. "You have told our pastor that Hannah is unfit to care for her younger brothers and sisters. You have asked the church to take them into its care."

"Yes." Mrs. Baylor's face was an angry red now. "If you want it plain, I accuse Hannah Mills of lying to cover up scandalous goings-on a week ago today and the night before."

Hannah stared openmouthed at Mrs. Baylor. Suddenly the room seemed very quiet. She was conscious of the clock ticking and Mrs. Baylor's breath whistling through her nostrils. Why had the woman brought such a monstrous accusation against her? She'd done Mrs. Baylor no harm. Then she began to remember.

A week ago she'd come back from Pine's Bridge. Eben told her Liddy was hurt. She had found her at the Baylors' shelter. Mrs. Baylor was angry she wouldn't say where she'd been. And then— She remembered her own voice refusing, none too politely. But that wasn't all, and it wasn't the real reason. Mrs. Baylor had wanted to keep Liddy, and she'd stood up against her. That was the real reason for the accusation.

Hannah knew this suddenly and surely, but she couldn't say it. She could only defend herself against Mrs. Baylor's complaints.

"Have you anything to say, Hannah?"

"Yes, sir." She took a deep breath. "I know what Mrs. Baylor has in mind. I did lie. I confess to that. But it wasn't to cover up anything wrong. I couldn't tell her then where I'd been. But there's no reason against it now. The day she's talking about I was riding to Pine's Bridge to warn Mr. Isaacs that De Lancey was planning to surprise him there and steal some cattle."

Mrs. Baylor's face swelled and grew even redder. "A fine tale to put on top of the first lie," she snorted. "Hannah has no horse. I say she was off with those infantry soldiers who were around that day. Why else would she lie?"

"It was Tamar Halstead's horse," Hannah explained.

Telling couldn't hurt Tamar now her father was gone. "She told me about De Lancey and lent me her mare, Queenie."

"A Tory girl! And you expect anyone to believe that?"

The moderator's eyes traveled from Mrs. Baylor to Hannah and then back. "Well, it's easy to find the right of this," he said. "We can ask Mr. Isaacs."

Mrs. Baylor looked surprised when Mr. Isaacs stepped into the room. "What business has he in our church affairs?" she asked belligerently. Then she changed her tone. "But so long as he's here, yes, do ask him. He will tell you Hannah lies when she talks about riding to Pine's Bridge to save his cattle."

Mr. Isaacs disregarded Mrs. Baylor and spoke to the elders. "If it hadn't been for Hannah, De Lancey's men would have taken sixty head I was driving to Peekskill for the army. Does that answer the accusation?"

Hannah walked over and stood by Mr. Isaacs. He put his arm around her. Mrs. Baylor glanced from face to face. They all looked set against her. Then she burst out, "Not quite. I want to know who she was meeting secretly the night before, when she left her little sister and brother all by themselves. My son Eben saw her pass our shelter."

From the safety of Mr. Isaacs' arm, Hannah replied. "I went to see Jacob. I had to talk to him."

"At midnight? Alone? Just to *talk*, Hannah?" Mrs. Baylor's voice was insinuating, her eyes triumphant.

Hannah felt her face grow hot. Mrs. Baylor was suggesting something shameful. She was trying to make out that she and Jacob had done something wrong. They'd talked about Elijah stealing, but how could she tell anyone that?

She stood tongue-tied and miserable, unable to say anything.

Then Mr. Isaacs' wrath rumbled through the room.

"It appears this is no longer a matter of your church. It appears Mrs. Baylor is accusing my son of misconduct. If that is so, let her be warned. A single word to that effect, either here or elsewhere, and I'll have her in the courts."

He bowed to the pastor and the elders. "If you have no further need of Hannah, may I take her home?"

"Yes, do," the moderator agreed. "Any further interest we have in this matter concerns only Mrs. Baylor. Good night, Hannah, my dear. You performed a real service to our country in riding to warn Mr. Isaacs about the Refugees."

The pastor came over and shook Mr. Isaacs by the hand and kissed Hannah on the forehead. He didn't say she needn't make public confession of her lie. He didn't say she could keep the children. But Hannah knew everything was all right.

Mr. Isaacs was so angry that Hannah hardly dared to speak to him while they were riding home. His anger was like the wrath of Moses, she thought, good and clean and strong. She'd never seen Jacob truly angry, but she suspected it would be the same with him. Hannah was glad it was dark when Mr. Isaacs let her off the horse. It made it easier to ask the question she'd been turning around in her mind.

"Mr. Isaacs, sir, will Jacob have to know what Mrs. Baylor said? I don't think I could look at him for shame if he knew."

Mr. Isaacs shook his head. "Mrs. Baylor knows enough to keep her mouth shut. I don't think anything more will be heard from her."

"Do you want to know why I went to see Jacob, sir?"

"No, Hannah. I don't. I'm sure there was no wrongdoing."

"When will he be back? Is he all right?"

Mr. Isaacs nodded. "He's attending to some business. If it turns out the way we hope, he'll be telling you about it soon." He pressed his heel against the horse, and it jogged off into the night. Hannah stood still a moment, listening to the clop-clop of its hooves.

Then she ran toward the shelter, shouting, "Elijah, Elijah, everything is all right! It's all over, and everything's all right."

CHAPTER 21

Every day, when she woke, Hannah wondered if Jacob was home. Whether she'd see him when she walked past the Isaacs' lot in the village. Mr. Isaacs was hiring one of the men who had helped on the cattle drive, and they already had the sills and crossbeams laid and the flooring down. When Jacob came, they'd be ready to start on the framing.

In their own lot, Hannah and Elijah had finished as much building as they could alone. Now Elijah was working for Mr. Slawson at the mill, while Hannah caught up with the weeds in the corn and potatoes and cabbage. There wouldn't be frost for a month, but they'd be ready for it when it came, with a place to store their winter vegetables. Andrew and Liddy were still at the farm. When Jacob was back, he and his father would ride them in on their horses.

When Jacob was back. A lot of Hannah's thought began that way these days. Then one evening he turned up at milking time, more excited than Hannah had ever seen him.

"Hannah! Elijah!" he called out before he even reached the shelter. "Your father is being exchanged!"

Pa being exchanged? At first Hannah couldn't believe she'd heard Jacob right. She was too scared she'd heard him wrong to say anything. But Elijah didn't doubt it for a minute.

"Pa's coming home!" he shouted. "Hannah, he's coming home! Don't just stand there with your mouth open. Pa's coming home!"

"It's true, Hannah," Jacob said, "only maybe I was too sudden in telling you."

Then Hannah did believe it. Suddenly she was laughing and crying, and shouting, "Pa's coming home!" right along with Elijah. For a while she didn't even ask Jacob how he knew about the exchange and how it had come about. When she did ask, Jacob told them, "The day of the cattle drive, we fished a man out of the Croton River after the Refugees had gone on. His horse was shot, and we thought the man was drowned until I saw him hanging onto some wood near shore. I took him prisoner."

He stopped there for a breath, but Elijah cried, "Jacob, go on!"

"Well, we decided to hold him for exchange with your father. De Lancey agreed to a private exchange and the British commissioner of prisoners in New York went along with it. That's how it happened."

"You went to see *De Lancey?* You did *that?*" Hannah's eyes shone with admiration.

"No, not me," Jacob replied. "That was Major Tallmadge. We met up with him and some other dragoons who had been off buying horses. My father went on to Peekskill with the cattle, and the dragoons and I took the prisoner south to Sheldon's outpost. Tallmadge arranged the exchange with De Lancey. I stayed at the outpost until it was all settled."

"Jacob, don't stop!" Hannah begged. "When will Pa be released? When will he get home?"

Jacob hesitated, looking serious. "I've got to tell you, Hannah. He's not too strong. He will need a wagon to ride in. Mr. Avery will lend us his to go down and get him. I got passes for you and Elijah and me to go through the lines. We will start day after tomorrow at daybreak from the farm."

"How sick is he?" Hannah asked apprehensively, while Elijah shouted, "Yipes! I've got to tell everyone Pa's getting home!"

He dashed off and they could hear him yelling the news as he went. Then Hannah asked again, "How sick is he? Is he going to get well?"

"His leg is bad," Jacob replied. "He can't fight again for a while. But he's not bed-sick according to what Tallmadge was told."

Hannah gave a deep sigh of relief. "Well, we can take care of him. We have a place ready. Oh, Jacob, how good it will be to have Pa home! I never really thought we'd see him again after I read that letter. How can we ever thank you?"

"No need to, Hannah. If you hadn't warned us in time to get over the bridge and take up the planks, that man wouldn't have been in the river to capture."

Hannah sat down on a stump to milk Magnolia, and Jacob leaned against a tree behind her, waiting for her to finish. After a while he said, "I'm sixteen next week."

"That's so, Jacob." She'd forgotten his birthday was so soon. "You going to join the militia?"

"Not the militia. The Continental army. I made up my mind while I was waiting word of your father's exchange."

"But, Jacob, that means you can be ordered anywhere in the country—we won't see you—or know—" She faltered and stopped.

"Well, I won't be going until after we finish the house," he replied. When she didn't say anything more, he went on. "Militia's important, Hannah. But the war can't be won just by defending close to home. To end it there has to be another kind of fighting, too. Men fighting together everywhere for the whole country. Don't you see that?"

"I guess I do." Hannah kept on milking, glad her back was to Jacob so he wouldn't know how she felt. There was a great big lump in her throat in spite of being so happy about Pa.

"Hannah?"

"Yes, Jacob?"

"Will you write when you can and let me know how things are with you? I'll be wanting to hear it from you—not just through Rachel."

Slowly, Hannah turned around until she faced him. Tears were running down her cheeks, but she wasn't shamed, now, that Jacob saw them.

"I'll do that," she promised. "I'll pray for you, too. Oh, Jacob, it's going to be hard to have you go!"

HISTORICAL NOTE

The main characters in *Summer of the Burning* are fictional, but the background is true. It is based on the eyewitness accounts of those who lived in Bedford during the Revolution, collected from 1844 through 1851 by John McLain Macdonald; on family stories of Bedford people, set down later by their descendants; on church records; and on military documents and journals.

All military officers ranking above captain are real, though I have made up conversation and minor action for them, consistent with their own writings and accounts of the time.

The attempt to capture the cattle Mr. Isaacs was driving to the army is fiction, but De Lancey did attack droves at Pine's Bridge many times. Taking up the planks was the common method of defending this bridge.

Because readers of this book will surely be reading other novels and also histories of the Revolution, they will come on some of these same officers and regiments again in other campaigns. To make them easier to recognize, when met, a few words of identification are added.

DE LANCEY. Colonel James De Lancey was a lower Westchester man, who in 1779 commanded a party of Refugees who fought without uniform and lived on what they plundered. In 1780 he became commander of the Westchester Refugee Corps, an organized Tory regiment.

MOYLAN. Colonel Stephen Moylan, an Irishman, commanded the Fourth Continental Dragoons from its organization around 1777 until the end of the war. The regiment was from Pennsylvania. But many of the men were Irish.

SHELDON. Colonel Elisha Sheldon commanded the Second Regiment of Continental Dragoons, organized in Connecticut, from December 1776 until the end of the war.

TARLETON. Lieutenant Colonel Banastre Tarleton commanded the British Legion, formed partly of American loyalists, from late in 1778 until the close of the war. A daring and brilliant officer, he was called Bloody Tarleton in Virginia. He was known as the Green Dragoon because of the color his legion wore instead of the scarlet of the 16th and 17th Light Dragoons.

TALLMADGE. Major Benjamin Tallmadge joined Sheldon's regiment in December 1776. From 1778 on, he also acted as head of Washington's spies in New York City and Long Island, a group called the Culper Ring. In 1781, he was called to serve at Washington's headquarters.